BARE-KNUCKLE MURDER

Skye Fargo looked at the man coming toward him. All three hundred pounds of him. Fargo, his back to the bar, moved his hand toward his Colt until he felt the pressure of a rifle barrel in his back.

Then the bartender reached over the bar and pulled Fargo's Colt from its holster.

"Now it'll be a fair fight," the barkeep said with a grin of sneering anticipation.

"You've a damn funny idea of fair," Fargo muttered and turned his eyes to the huge form closing in on him. This would be no fair fight. It wasn't supposed to be any kind of contest at all.

Not when the Trailsman had only his bare hands to stop a man mountain bent on naked murder . . .

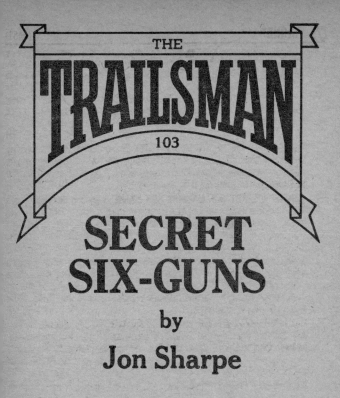

THE

TRAILSMAN

103

SECRET
SIX-GUNS

by

Jon Sharpe

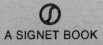

A SIGNET BOOK

SIGNET
Published by the Penguin Group
Penguin Books USA Inc., 375 Hudson Street,
New York, New York 10014, U.S.A.
Penguin Books Ltd, 27 Wrights Lane,
London W8 5TZ, England
Penguin Books Australia Ltd, Ringwood,
Victoria, Australia
Penguin Books Canada Ltd, 2801 John Street,
Markham, Ontario, Canada L3R 1B4
Penguin Books (N.Z.) Ltd, 182-190 Wairau Road,
Auckland 10, New Zealand

Penguin Books Ltd, Registered Offices:
Harmondsworth, Middlesex, England

First published by Signet, an imprint of Penguin Books USA Inc.

First Printing, July, 1990
10 9 8 7 6 5 4 3 2 1

REGISTERED TRADEMARK—MARCA REGISTRADA

Printed in the United States of America

PUBLISHER'S NOTE
This is a work of fiction. Names, characters, places, and incidents either are the produc
of the author's imagination or are used fictitiously, and any resemblance to actual
persons, living or dead, events, or locales is entirely coincidental.

The Trailsman

Beginnings . . . they bend the tree and they mark the man. Skye Fargo was born when he was eighteen. Terror was his midwife, vengeance his first cry. Killing spawned Skye Fargo, ruthless, cold-blooded murder. Out of the acrid smoke of gunpowder still hanging in the air, he rose, cried out a promise never forgotten.

The Trailsman, they began to call him, all across the West: searcher, scout, hunter, the man who could see where others only looked, his skills for hire but not his soul, the man who lived each day to the fullest, yet trailed each tomorrow. Skye Fargo, the Trailsman, the seeker who could take the wildness of a land and the wanting of a woman and make them his own.

*Idaho, 1860, where the Bitterroot Mountains
spilled their wildness down from
the north country . . .*

1

The big man's lake-blue eyes were narrowed as they peered hard through the thick foliage of the mountain slope. He wondered, for a moment, if the morning mists and the dense cover of Rocky Mountain maple had made his eyes play tricks on him. But then the horse and rider appeared again, below him, halfway down the mountainside slope. The rider, dressed in a black cape, black trousers, and a wide-brimmed black hat that completely hid his face, moved along a narrow path that crossed the middle of the slope. Skye Fargo's eyes flicked to the steep, tree-covered slopes that surrounded him.

The trail he rode wandered along one side of four slopes that surrounded a deep hollow, lush, thick land of blue spruce, hackberry, and hawthorn as well as Rocky Mountain maple. Until the strange, black-clad rider had come into view, he had seen only moose, white-tailed deer, black bear, and the ever-present raccoons. These hills, part of the Bitterroot Mountain Range, were a wild and untamed place. The animals belonged, part of the wildness, integral to the land, but the rider all in black had been a sudden, jarring note.

Fargo watched the figure move slowly along the narrow trail below. He began to move the Ovaro down the slope, drawn by curiosity more than anything else, as the rider below appeared and disappeared through the thick tree cover, still only a distant figure. But the man suddenly halted and Fargo saw him draw a rifle from beneath the voluminous black cape, half-turn, and raise the gun toward the slope to his left. Fargo's eyes flicked to the slope in time to see a horseman in a red-checked shirt halfway up the hillside on a narrow deer trail. The rifle shot reverberated from the four hillsides and echoed back and forth into the hollow as Fargo watched the man in the red-checked shirt topple from his horse, arms flying into the air.

The Trailsman wrenched his eyes back to the path below to see that the black-clad figure had left the path and was already racing downhill. "Damn," he swore, and sent the Ovaro down the hillside in pursuit, confident of the magnificent black-and-white horse's strength and surefootedness. He saw the black-clad rider swerve into a thick stand of blue spruce halfway down the hillside. The rider vanished and came into sight again where the spruce ended, and raced into a dense forest of hackberry.

Fargo followed, slowing as he threaded his way through the tangle of closely growing trees. He spotted the broken ends of the low branches where the other horseman had raced through. He suddenly reined to a halt. The trail, such as it was, had vanished with the horse and rider. Fargo's frown deepened as he scanned every patch of the thick forest. The forest floor was too cushioned with bristlegrass and broom moss to show hoofprints. If the rider had dismounted and carefully led his horse, he could have avoided leaving a trail of snapped branch ends, Fargo thought, but then he'd have to move very slowly and carefully. The Trailsman urged the pinto forward again, his eyes sweeping the forest in front of him until he finally reined to a halt. He'd have caught up to the black-clad figure by now if the man were leading his horse. With a snorted curse, Fargo turned and went back to where the trail ended.

He pushed through the forest to his left this time, again scanning the wooded brush for any sign, and had to rein to a halt when he found himself facing the side of a high hill. Part flat rock and part brush-covered earth, the hill rose steeply, almost vertically, the rock sections covered with climbing moss and the earth with tough mountain shrub. Martens and pine squirrels could climb the steep side but not much else. Once again he turned the Ovaro in a tight circle and rode back to where the trail ended. He rode to the right now, into the forest. He'd gone perhaps a thousand yards when he came to a wide, slow-moving stream that softened the earth for at least a half-dozen yards on both sides.

The Ovaro's hoofprints immediately appeared in the softened ground, but they were the only prints there. No one had come this way, Fargo saw. No one had crossed the stream, either on horseback or on foot. His lips drawn back in a grimace and a frown on his brow, he returned to where he had entered the hackberry, paused, and then steered the pinto up the opposite slope. When he reached the deer trail where the killer's target had toppled from his horse, he stared at the ground. There was no one there. No slain form in a checked shirt, no victim, nothing.

Fargo dismounted and dropped to one knee as he

studied the ground. He saw no bloodstains, no marks of a wounded man dragging himself away. The man had disappeared as completely as the black-clad rifleman. If he had left tracks, he'd had time to cover them.

Fargo rose and pulled himself onto the pinto. "Dammit," he swore aloud. He wasn't one for seeing things, for wild imaginings. Nor did he put much store in ghosts and apparitions.

Above all else, he was the Trailsman, the one who found trails, not lost them. He swung the Ovaro around and returned to the narrow pathway he had been riding when he first saw the black-clad figure. He paused to take one more long glance at the slopes and the hollow in the center, but nothing moved. The mountainsides had returned to their stillness and the morning mists were all but gone now. The frown still clung to him as he moved the pinto on along the path and once again followed the directions in the letter in his jacket pocket. "At the north tip of St. Joseph's forest you'll come to four high hills—Blue Spruce Hills the natives call them—with a deep hollow in the center. Go around the hollow, and after the north slope the land will level off. Keep riding north until you reach Twin Table Rock. Take the path to the right and you'll come to the house."

The strange incident with the black-clad rider still stabbing at him, Fargo guided the Ovaro along the narrow pathway as it wound its way to the north slope of the four high hills. When he finally emerged on the other side of the slope, he saw the land quickly level itself, almost in a high plateau with heavy stands of box elder and some spruce. The narrow pathway around the slopes had been difficult riding, and the morning sun grew hot. When he spied a tiny, bubbling spring,

12

he dismounted and let the Ovaro drink and rest in the shade of a wide-branched box elder. Fargo sat down against the gray-brown bark of the tree trunk and pulled the letter from his pocket.

"My old friend Fargo," he read once again. "I have something that desperately calls for the talents of the Trailsman. The enclosed money is half your fee in advance. Please come. Doc Emerson."

The rest of the letter had contained directions, but the few opening lines had brought back an instant flood of memories when he had first read them. He smiled as the memories rushed back again now. He looked forward to meeting Oscar Emerson again. Doc Emerson was one of the good people, a man who had proved himself a man of dedication. Their first meeting back in Kansas Territory was indelibly stamped in his mind, Fargo realized. The Bramdon family, all eight of them, had come down with the fever. Some neighbors suspected smallpox and everyone was frightened. The doctors in the nearby towns all developed excuses why they couldn't come, some honest reasons, some not so honest.

But Doc Emerson came. He came and stayed and worked day and night. Fargo recalled how, at the doc's plea, he had ridden fifty miles through Pawnee country for a special serum. But it had ended well. Doc Emerson's efforts saved everyone but a small child, and when it was all over, Fargo and the doctor had shared a bottle of bourbon.

Fargo smiled as he pushed away his memories and pocketed the letter. He rose, called the Ovaro, and moved northward again at a slow trot. Twin Table Rock was exactly what the name implied—two long slabs of rock side by side that resembled two giant tables. The right-hand path led him some two miles before he came to a small log house with a stone foundation. But when he reined to a halt in front of the house, it was not Doc Emerson's balding, slightly portly figure that stepped outside to meet him. Instead, he found himself looking at a young woman in a plain beige cotton dress. He noted her brown hair trimmed short, eyes almost the exact same shade of brown as her hair, and even features in a face that was pretty in a plain way. He took in a slender body put together with a kind of neatness, nothing shouting out at one, breasts, hips, legs, everything modest yet fitting together with trim balance.

"Skye Fargo. I've been waiting for you," she said.

"How do you know who I am?" he asked with mild surprise.

"Doc Emerson told me about you. He described you and that magnificent Ovaro of yours," the young woman said. "I'm Emily Holden."

He noted she had a directness about her, the brown eyes steady and observing. He swung from the horse and Emily Holden pushed the door of the house open. "Please come in," she said, and Fargo followed her into a wide living room with a fireplace at one end and modest furnishings; there was a bright quilted rug on the floor.

"The doc out on a call?" Fargo asked as Emily closed the door.

"No," the young woman said, and Fargo picked up the tiny line of tension that tightened the corners of her mouth. "I've the kettle boiling. Would you like some coffee?" she asked.

"Sounds fine," he said, and watched her hurry into the kitchen, admiring her narrow hips and firm, round little rear, which seemed as neat as the rest of her. She returned in moments with two mugs of hot coffee, rich and flavorfull. He took the time to enjoy the bracing brew.

"Please sit down," Emily Holden said, and lowered herself onto the edge of a leather sofa. She held her knees together, he noted as he took the chair opposite her. Not a primness, but a kind of contained control to her, he decided as his eyes moved across her face again. Only the slightest touch of rouge, thin eyebrows carefully plucked, a small, straight nose, and nice but slightly thin lips. His first reaction had been right, he thought: pretty in a plain way. And yet, there was something more to her. It was in the steady directness of her brown eyes, something not unlike a banked fire. Again, he saw the tiny lines tighten her lips as she spoke. "Doc Emerson isn't here," Emily said. "He didn't send you the letter."

Fargo frowned as he took another sip of the coffee. "Who did?" he asked.

"I did," Emily said.

"And signed his name to it," Fargo said, and she nodded.

"I was afraid you wouldn't come if it had been from me."

"Why didn't Doc Emerson send it?"

"Because he's disappeared," Emily said with quiet firmness. Fargo frowned back. "That's right, disappeared, simply vanished," she said.

Fargo's frown stayed. "Disappearing seems a popular thing around here," he muttered.

"What do you mean?" Emily asked quickly.

"Nothing important," Fargo said, brushing aside the query. "Tell me about Doc Emerson. What do you mean he just disappeared?"

"Exactly that," Emily answered. "He went to town. He has a small office there. He never came back."

15

"You talk to anybody about it?"

"Of course," Emily Holden said with a trace of annoyed impatience at the question. "I've talked to everybody, Mayor Frey, Myron Beezer, Harvey Stoller, Harriet Tilson, everybody."

"And what'd they tell you?"

"Nobody knows what happened to him. Nobody saw him that day. Nobody knows anything. They did a lot of wringing their hands and some searching, but he's still missing," Emily said.

"Maybe he went off someplace and fell into a gulley. This mountain country is pretty damn rugged."

"He wasn't going anywhere except to the office, and the searching never found him," Emily said.

He gave her a narrowed glance. "You saying something else?"

"I'm saying he's missing and something's not right about it," Emily said, her voice rising a notch.

"But you don't know what's not right."

"No, not yet."

"Who's Emily Holden?" Fargo asked. "What's her stake in this? Just curiosity?"

"I'm a nurse. I worked with Doc Emerson, but it was more than that. He was like a father to me. He put me through nurse training, worked with me, guided me, took me under his wing. He was a wonderful man," Emily said.

"I know that."

"Then you'll find him?" she said quickly.

"I can't promise that."

"Trying is all I ask."

"I'll want to know more than you've told me—details, little things, meaningless things that might suddenly mean a lot," he said.

"Whatever I can tell you," Emily said, and Fargo

let thoughts turn in his mind for a long moment. A man didn't just vanish into thin air, he grunted, despite the black-clad rider and his victim. Not a man such as Doc Emerson. There had to be reasons, and he sensed there was a lot Emily Holden hadn't given voice to yet. He broke off thoughts and met her steady, waiting eyes, anxiety in their brown depths.

"You've got a deal," he said, and watched Emily break into a smile that was part relief and part delight. It was the first time he'd seen her smile, he realized, and it brightened her seriousness with an almost little-girl warmth.

She rose quickly, impulsively, and brushed his cheek with a quick, fleeting touch of a kiss. "Thank you," she said. "I was afraid you might think me a little fool unwilling to listen to what others have said."

"We'll see about that," he told her.

2

"You'll stay here, won't you? There's Doc's room, my room, and a guest room," she said.

"Maybe."

"Where else would you stay?" Emily frowned.

"Depends what I find and what I do."

She let her lips purse in thought for a moment. "I suppose so," she muttered. "Meanwhile, stable your horse in the barn out back and we can talk about all those things you want to ask me."

"Later. I want to visit town first. Sort of get the measure of the place," Fargo said.

"I'll go along."

"No," he said more sharply than he'd intended, and saw a wry smile edge the young woman's lips.

"Say what you mean, Skye Fargo," she remarked, and he questioned with a frown. "You want to talk, ask questions, and you don't want me around. Because you want to take the measure of me as well as the town."

He allowed a slow smile. The directness of her brown eyes was confirmed by her tongue, he noted. "Maybe in time. For now, I'm not going to talk to a soul. I just want to ride through and look for myself."

Emily shrugged. "No matter. It's your right," she said, dismissing the subject. "Go past Twin Table Rock, stay on the road, and you'll come to the town."

"It's got a name, I take it," he said.

"Mountain Parasol, but everybody just calls it Parasol," she said, and walked to the door with him. "I'll have dinner ready when you come back," she said, and he saw her watch him ride away with her thoughtful stare.

Fargo rode unhurriedly, passed Twin Table Rock, and found the road beyond a succession of climbs and dips as the mountain terrain surrounded it on both sides. His eyes scanned the mountains that pressed to the edge of the road, heavy, thick, and throbbing with their own vitality.

These mountains were Nez Percé country, and they were just as hostile as when the early French trappers explored the country. It was those early French mountain men who gave the Nez Percé the name that stayed for all the white men that followed. The Pierced Nose people, those trappers had called them, for their practice of wearing pieces of shell through their nostrils. They had another name once, Fargo mused, but he didn't know it. Never met anyone who did. They once fought on the plains, he'd heard. But now they were part of this mountain fastness. Many used the Nez Percé word for this land—Idaho—the Indian word for the place where the sun rolls down the mountains. But officially, it was still part of Oregon Territory.

He saw a number of trails that cut through the heavily foliaged hills, some hardly more than deep trails but some wider, clearly cut through by hand. He decided to explore one of the widest. He turned and rode up into a passage where the marks of wagon wheels were still on the ground. The passage narrowed some, but it was clearly a trail carved by those out to cross through the mountains by wagon. He'd climbed almost two miles and glimpsed pieces of the trail still visible in the distance. He wondered if it indeed went all the way through these deep mountains, or did it peter out someplace surrounded by the bones of those who'd learned the price of failure in this wild country. But he'd no time nor desire to follow it farther, and was about to turn back when a man appeared in front of him, sitting astride a thin, sway-backed mount. Long black hair stuck out from below the brim of a torn hat and he held an old Kentucky mountain rifle in his hands as he peered out of a lined, stern face.

"What you be doing here, mister?" the man growled.

"Riding. Looking around," Fargo said blandly.

"No wagon passing through. No tools, so you're no miner. No traps, so you be no trapper. You be snooping," the man said, and Fargo saw the dark wildness in his eyes. "I don't allow snooping here."

"Easy, friend," Fargo said placatingly. The man held the rifle in his hands, ready to swing it around instantly. But it was a heavy, cumbersome piece, clumsy to handle and slow to fire, Fargo knew. He dropped his hand to rest on the butt of the big Colt at his side. "I didn't know a man couldn't ride these mountains," he said, again keeping his voice calm.

"If he's got a reason. You be plain snooping," the man said, his voice rising.

"Riding, not snooping," Fargo tried again.

But the wild-eyed man wasn't about to be placated. "No, snooping. You be snooping, nothing else," he said.

Fargo grimaced. The man seemed a mental case, not a target for a shooting confrontation, and he tried again to reach him. "Now, how do you know I'm snooping? How can you be so sure?" he asked.

"No traps. No pack mule. No miner's tools. Hell, not even a fishing pole. Snooping, that's all you be, and that'll cost you, mister." Fargo saw the man's hands tighten as he started to swing the rifle around to fire. "Damn," he muttered as he drew the Colt in one smooth, unbroken motion, almost too quick for the eye to follow. The man had swung the heavy rifle almost fully around, his finger tightening on the trigger, but fast and slow were suddenly measured in split seconds. The Colt barked and the man let out a groaning cough as he flew backward from his horse, the rifle falling from his hands.

Fargo, another oath on his lips, moved the pinto forward to stare down at the figure on the ground, his chest a deep hole that gushed red.

The man had appeared from the trees at his left, and Fargo moved the Ovaro through the foliage in that direction and followed a narrow opening that appeared. He pushed aside mostly blue-spruce branches, edged his way past a few hackberry, and finally came to a sod house with a roof of twigs and leaves, one corner crumbling away. He dismounted and peered inside to find a shambles of old clothes, half-eaten bits of food, and a torn mattress. The man had plainly been some sort of hermit, a recluse with a taste for shooting those he fancied trespassers in his domain. Fargo poked through the sod hut for a few moments more, found nothing with a name on it, and returned to the Ovaro and the road to town.

The hostile recluse had given him no choice but to shoot, but the distaste of the action clung to him as he rode. Dense mountain country always attracted solitary misfits, some harmless, some dangerous. But these mountains seemed to have more than the usual share of strange incidents, Fargo pondered as his thoughts returned to the black-clad rider. Finally he came into sight of the distant buildings and spurred the Ovaro into a trot. He'd seen these mountain towns often enough, isolated little enclaves that seemed to spring up as a mushroom appears on a log. Mostly they were more way stations than towns, existing for trappers, hunters, miners, mountain men, and those travelers who braved crossing the mountains. They were towns fashioned of sheds and storehouses, trading posts, and of course, the ever-present dance hall. In the bitter cold of winter they served as a refuge, for only a few of the hardiest mountain men stayed out during the winter blizzards.

But when Fargo reached the first buildings of Mountain Parasol, his reflections gave way to a frown as he saw a neat row of houses, some with picket fences outside. He continued into town and slowed to look at two women in a surrey driving down the main street, both well-dressed and wearing flowered hats, both in their early forties, he guessed. A little farther on, he passed another three neat houses with flowers in window boxes. There were a few storage sheds, and he passed the saloon, the words DRINKS and DOLLS painted over the double doors. He saw a good number of Owensboro mountain wagons and pack mules, but instead of the shabby trading post he expected, he came to a neat general store. Two women emerged with bolts of fabric under their arms as he passed, both fairly young.

The frown dug deeper into his brow as he came to a freshly painted building with the words: TOWN MEETING HALL, painted on the outside wall. He rode on and saw a boot shop and a barber shop and drew to a halt when he came to a bank.

He stared at the building, saw a well-dressed man emerge and two men in woodsmen clothes carry a small wooden chest into the building. He continued to stare at the bank until he finally turned away and rode to the other end of town and back again. There remained plenty of mountain wagons and burly men on the street, but he had expected that. It was the rest of Parasol that astonished him. It took an established and sizable town in a proper location to have itself a bank and a general store. Yet Parasol, tucked away high in the Bitterroot Mountains, had both. Which made it the damnedest mountain town he had ever seen, Fargo murmured to himself as he rode back through town.

He rode from town with the purple of dusk beginning to drift down from the surrounding mountains and reached Doc Emerson's after dark. He took the Ovaro into the stable, where two ordinary-looking mounts were in their stalls; he unsaddled the pinto and put him into a stall with a bucket of oats.

Emily had the door of the house open when he reached it, and the fragrance of a stewing fowl in herbs reminded him how hungry he was. He entered to see Emily had changed to a dark-blue dress with a square neckline. The garment, folded against her neat, trim body, with her short hair brushed back, made him think of a young girl dressed up for the first time, a certain appealing awkwardness to her.

"Didn't expect you'd be dressing for dinner," he said.

"I do when I can. Doc Emerson and I agreed it was a way to keep in touch with civilized living up in these mountains," Emily said, and gestured to a chair drawn up at a table set with wicker place mats.

"Parasol looked pretty damn civilized," Fargo said. "A lot more so than I'd expected."

"Yes, it is, and they hold town socials, but Doc and I were never invited," Emily said as Fargo sat down at the table and she poured a glass of wine for him from a carafe.

"Give me some background. How did Doc Emerson come to settle down here?"

"He was contacted by Mayor Frey and the president of the bank, Myron Beezer. They wanted a town doctor, a man who'd serve just Parasol and the outlying areas. They guaranteed a base salary plus whatever fees he charged his patients. The doc said it was unlike any offer he ever heard of, and he took it. He needed a nurse and brought me along," Emily said.

"How long have you been here?" Fargo asked as Emily served dinner.

"Almost two years," she said.

"Was Doc Emerson happy here?"

"Yes. In fact, he used to say that the town fascinated him," Emily said.

"How'd he mean that?"

"He never explained more."

"They try to get a new doc yet?"

"No, but they asked me to go on sick calls until they hire another doctor."

"You been doing that?"

"As best I can. I sure can't fill Doc Emerson's shoes," Emily said.

"They know you're not happy with the searching they did?" Fargo asked.

"I've said as much," Emily sniffed.

Fargo let himself study the young woman as he finished the meal. There was no flightiness to her, he saw again. She seemed hardly the kind to go off in hysterical imaginings. Yet, so far, nothing added up to anything more than a possible accident. "Seems to me you have to face the fact that he could have gotten a summons, gone out by himself, and had an accident on one of those mountain trails. Some are pretty damn treacherous," Fargo said.

"No, that didn't happen," she said firmly.

"How can you be so sure? He didn't take you along on every call, did he?"

"No, he didn't," she admitted. "But he had an appointment book in his office in town. He marked down every appointment and call he went on. It was something he always did. He was scrupulous about it. When I went to his office to look for him, I looked at the appointment book. There was nothing on it."

"All right, so he didn't go out on a call. Maybe he just went for a ride by himself. There are a lot of wild characters in these hills. I met up with one this afternoon," Fargo said.

"Thin-faced man with wild black hair and carrying an old Kentucky rifle?" Emily asked, and he nodded with a frown. "You met Ernie. That's all they call him. He roams the hills around Parasol, guarding the town."

"Not anymore he doesn't," Fargo said, and told her what had happened.

She frowned into space for a moment when he finished. "He was a little mad, they said," she murmured.

"More than a little, I'd say," Fargo remarked. "They knew about him and never did anything?"

"They seemed content to just let him be," Emily said.

"Guarding the town," Fargo grunted. "Against what?"

"Who knows? Whatever was inside his crazy head," Emily said. "But he wouldn't have hurt Doc Emerson, if that's what you're thinking. He knew the doc. And he knew me. He never bothered us."

"So it seems."

"You said something else earlier today. You said disappearing seems a thing around here. What did you mean?" Emily asked.

He told her about the black-clad rider and his victim. "How's that for a fine story?" he asked when he finished.

"You had a dream," she said, and he frowned back. "Some dreams can be so vivid you think they really happened. I've seen patients who experienced that."

"I'm not a patient, nursie, and I know a dream from the real thing," Fargo growled.

"How do you explain it?"

"I don't, dammit," he snapped. "I just know what it wasn't."

She fixed one of her steady, direct stares at him. "Whatever it was, it has nothing to do with Doc Emerson's disappearance. That's what I care about."

Fargo smiled, the message hardly subtle. "The meal was real good," he said, turn-away words. Her tiny smile told him she recognized them as that.

"I'll show you the guest room," she said. "I'm sure you could use a good bed after riding all day." He followed her into a small, neat room with a bed against one wall, a small dresser, and a night table with a lamp burning on low atop it. "There's a well with fresh water at the side of the house. Good night, Fargo," she said, paused before turning away. "You plan to go back to town tomorrow?" she asked.

"This time I'll be asking questions."

"You'll be back for supper, then."

"Can't say. Depends on what I turn up. Don't wait,"

he said. "Meanwhile, you keep thinking. You might remember something that would help."

"If only I could," Emily said as she walked away.

Fargo watched her go. Emily Holden had a quiet attractiveness and a quiet determination, he noted again. Yet perhaps she was very wrong about her suspicions. Maybe he'd find that out in the morning, he told himself as he undressed, stretched out, and enjoyed the luxury of a good bed. He turned out the lamp and let sleep rush over him.

The night passed all too quickly and he was washed and dressed when Emily appeared, all but lost in a long, billowy nightgown. He waved to her as he hurried to the stable and saddled the Ovaro. She was still in the doorway, watching, as he rode away, still wanting to go with him.

Fargo put the horse into a canter and rode toward town, again scanning the dense mountains on both sides as he rode. He fought away the impulse to turn off and go back to the deep hollow in the hills where he had seen the rider in black. But he would return for another look, he knew, if only out of a sense of curiosity. Riders didn't vanish on him, to say nothing of their victims.

The morning activities of the town were in full swing when Fargo reached Parasol. He slowed and let the horse walk along the main street. Trappers were loading burros with supplies and others were stocking mountain wagons. Two women were busy talking outside the town meeting hall, one large, brown-haired and cloaked in a pink dress, the other smaller, younger, and less eye-catching. The two women turned to him as he halted and tipped his hat. "Pardon me, ladies, but would I find the mayor's office inside the Town Meeting Hall?" he asked.

"Yes, but Mayor Frey's not there," the large woman in pink answered, a touch of imperiousness in her voice. "He's gone to a meeting at the bank with Myron Beezer."

"Much obliged." Fargo smiled.

"Just passing through?" the woman asked. "I'm Harriet Tilson, president of the Parasol Ladies Association."

"I'm not sure, yet. This is a right proper town you have here," Fargo said.

"Yes, we like it. We don't get too many strangers. Most of our visitors are mountain men from the region," Harriet Tilson said. "And of course, the ocassional settler wagons passing through. You're obviously not either," she added with an appraising glance.

"That's right." Fargo smiled and moved the Ovaro forward. He felt Harriet Tilson's eyes following him as he rode on. An inquisitive woman, he thought, and drew to a halt when he reached the bank. He draped the Ovaro's reins over the hitching post and strolled into the bank, taking in the room with one quick glance. A teller counted out money to a man across from him while another customer waited in line. A smaller room behind the main part of the bank held a woman who sat behind a desk with an open ledger in front of her. A third, inner office followed the alcove where the woman sat, its door closed. As he stepped toward the closed door, the woman rose at once.

"May I help you?" she asked, and he took in a small, tight face that seemed old beyond its years, brown hair pulled back tightly, a high-buttoned dull-brown dress over a thin shape.

"Came to see Mayor Frey. I understand he's here," Fargo said.

"Yes, with Mr. Beezer, our president," she said. "I'm Lucille Todman, Mr. Beezer's bookkeeper."

"Fargo . . . Skye Fargo," he said.

"What is it you want with Mayor Frey?" the woman asked.

"Got a few questions for him," Fargo said casually just as the door opened and he saw three men come out of the inner office. Two were well-dressed in jackets, trousers, and neckties, the third one was tall with a heavy beard, torn hat, riding Levi's, and a gun belt. He carried a heavy, canvas money bag, a lock at the top and any markings on it obliterated with black paint.

"Mayor Frey's the gentleman in the dark-blue suit," Lucille said. "That's Mr. Beezer in gray."

Fargo nodded and watched the banker cross the room to where a six-foot-tall iron safe took up most of one wall. He opened the door and the roughly dressed man swung the heavy money bag into the safe as Myron Beezer smiled approvingly. One hand on the other man's shoulder, he turned to his bookkeeper as he pushed the door of the safe shut.

"Lucille, go over to Sam at the barber shop. Make an appointment for Mr. Smith for tomorrow morning. He'll want the full treatment," the banker said.

"Yes, sir," Lucille Todman said, and gestured to the big man with the lake-blue eyes. "This person's waiting to see Mayor Frey," she said.

Fargo watched the mayor turn and come toward him; he saw a sharp face, a hooked nose, and black hair carefully combed to one side. As the third man hurried away, the banker hurried after Mayor Frey, a slightly portly figure with a round face that also held a pair of cold, probing eyes. Fargo had the strange feeling that both men felt slightly uncomfortable in the suits they wore.

"New customer?" Fargo said to the banker.

"Yes," Myron Beezer said, allowed a broad smile to follow the single word. "But you're here to see the mayor."

"Got some questions you can both answer," Fargo said.

"Questions?" Mayor Frey echoed with an inquiring frown.

"About Doc Emerson," Fargo said casually, but caught the surprise that flashed through both men's faces.

"What about Doc Emerson?" Mayor Frey frowned.

"I hear he disappeared," Fargo said, keeping his voice casual.

"Yes, a tragedy," the mayor said. "He went off on a call, apparently, and just disappeared. It's not hard to do in these mountains."

"We searched for him, couldn't find a sign of him anywhere," the banker put in. "He could've slipped, gone into one of the gulleys or ravines. Or maybe the Nez Percé took him. Anything's possible."

"How did you come to know about this tragedy, Fargo?" the mayor asked.

"I didn't. Emily Holden called me in," Fargo said mildly.

"What?" Mayor Frey exploded as both men's jaws dropped in unison.

"She wanted an expert. Some call me the Trails-man," Fargo said.

"That damn-fool woman," the mayor swore, and exchanged quick frowns with Myron Beezer. "She'd no cause to do that."

"She seems to think so." Fargo half-shrugged.

"We told her we'd searched all over. She just refuses to believe he's gone," the mayor said.

"Now, Harold, we've discussed this," the banker said soothingly. "The poor thing's in a bad way. Doc Emerson's disappearance seemed to send her off the deep end."

Mayor Frey frowned into space for a moment and then shook his head vigorously. "Yes, I'd forgotten how we talked about that," he said, and turned back to Fargo. "I hope she paid you to come all this way, Fargo. You've really made a trip for nothing."

"She paid me," Fargo said, and kept his face expressionless as he saw the nervousness in the two men's faces, the mayor less able to hide it than the banker.

"That's good, because you've made a wasted trip. We searched carefully. He just disappeared," Mayor Frey said.

"I thought I'd just look around some for myself, seeing as I'm here," Fargo said.

"Look all you like. You won't find anything," Mayor Frey insisted.

"I'm not going to wander around the mountains. I'm figuring on talking to people," Fargo said.

"Talking to people?" Myron Beezer frowned.

"Maybe somebody saw him that day. Maybe somebody knows where he was going. When you look for a trail, you have to start someplace," Fargo said mildly.

"There's no need to bother folks with a lot of questions. We asked everyone already. The whole thing upset folks. Nobody knows anything," the mayor said.

"Maybe you missed somebody." Fargo smiled pleasantly but drew only a hard frown from Mayor Frey.

"Always a possibility," Myron Beezer put in almost soothingly.

"You have a sheriff here in Parasol?" Fargo asked.

"No," Mayor Frey answered. "Every town has a little trouble now and then, but we've seen no need for a sheriff."

Fargo nodded, well aware that there were many more towns without a sheriff than with one in the territories. "I'll be stopping by again, probably," he said, and strolled from the bank. He took the Ovaro by the cheek strap and led the horse at a walk as he started through town. He kept the frown inside him as he strolled along the main street. Both men had had a very definite reaction to the mention of Doc Emerson. The mayor had been the more hostile. Did he just resent Emily not accepting his conclusions? Was he a man who simply resented being disbelieved? Or was he nervous about something? Myron Beezer had been just as adamant about Doc Emerson's disappearance, but not as resentful of questions. Or did he just hide his resentment better?

Neither man had offered any cooperation. Neither had volunteered to tell him where they had searched or for how long. Neither offered to help him. But both had been angry at Emily Holden for bringing him here. Too angry. Myron Beezer had intimated that the event had unhinged her. Mayor Frey had called her a damn-fool woman. So far he had not seen either accusation borne out in Emily Holden. But then, he hadn't really seen enough of her to know, he reminded himself. He snapped off thoughts, deciding to table further speculation for the moment as he halted in front of the general store. A man leaned against the side of the store's open door, a white shopkeeper's apron over trousers and a striped shirt. Fargo took in a heavy face with a dark stubble of a beard, thick arms and heavy hands, a squat body and square chest—a man who seemed more an ox-cart driver than a merchant.

"Greetings, friend. The name's Fargo, Skye Fargo." The Trailsman smiled.

"Ben Stoppard," the storekeeper said.

"Maybe you can help me," Fargo began. "I'm trying to find out what happened to Doc Emerson. Did you happen to see him on the day he disappeared?"

The man's brows came together in a frown as he stared back and took in the broad-shouldered stranger. "Didn't see him," he answered after a moment, his voice flat.

"Too bad," Fargo said pleasantly. "I'll have to keep asking around."

"Who are you, mister? What makes you so interested in Doc Emerson?" Stoppard growled.

"Emily Holden hired me to find out what happened to him," Fargo answered.

"Hell, she knows what happened to him. Everybody knows what happened to him. He went into the mountains, made a mistake, and ended up at the bottom of one of those gorges," Ben said.

"That seems to be the general opinion," Fargo said. "She's not satisfied with it."

"The hell with her, then," the man said.

"Thanks for your time." Fargo nodded and walked on to halt a dozen feet down the street where the red-and-white striped barber pole stood outside a storefront.

A man came to the door, a young face despite the lines around the eyes, a mustache cup in one hand. "Yes, sir? Shave? Haircut? Bath?" he said. "Sam's Barber Shop offers all the comforts a man needs except a woman." He smiled broadly and Fargo returned his smile.

"Just a few questions," Fargo said. "About Doc Emerson."

The man's smile vanished as a veil of caution slid over his face. "What about Doc Emerson?"

"I'm trying to find out about his disappearance. I'm looking for somebody who saw him or talked to him that day," Fargo said.

"Keep looking," the barber said, a new sullenness in his voice.

"Much obliged." Fargo nodded and watched the man abruptly turn and stalk into the shop. The Trailsman grunted as he walked on until he came to a stop again, this time in front of the meeting hall. He left the Ovaro untethered outside as he went in to find a large, empty room with a few dozen chairs stacked at one side. The closed door of another room beckoned a few feet away, and he read the sign on the door: HARVEY STOLLER, CHAIRMAN, TOWN BOARD. He knocked at the door.

"Come in," a voice answered.

Fargo pushed the door open to find a small room, a table in the center and a man seated behind the table, two ledger books spread out before him. The man rose, tall, lanky of face and figure, middle-aged with a receding hairline. "I was expecting Myron Beezer," he said. "What can I do for you, stranger?"

"Emily Holden hired me to look into Doc Emerson's disappearance," Fargo said, the words falling automatically from his lips now.

Stoller frowned back. "Is that so?" he murmured.

"I'm trying to find someone who might've seen him the day he vanished," Fargo said.

"Sorry, can't help you," Stoller said. "You should talk to Mayor Frey about this."

"I did. Myron Beezer, too. They weren't much help, so I'm asking around."

"Guess you'll have to keep on asking," the man said. "I didn't see him that day."

"Got any ideas who might've seen him?" Fargo queried. "I'm told the doc was a very well-known figure in town."

"He was, but I don't know who might've talked to him that day," the man answered. "Guess you'll just have to keep asking."

"Guess so," Fargo said. "Thanks for your time."

Harvey Stoller nodded as Fargo walked from the room and returned to the pinto waiting outside. He walked on, asked the same questions of Tom Riley, who ran a boot repair shop; Abe Henderson, who sold packhorses and donkeys; and Dennis Warren, who owned a storage shed. But his questions received the same curt answers, even from those he halted walking the street. He'd neared the end of town when he saw the large woman in the pink dress again, this time snipping leaves from a bush outside a neat house with window boxes filled with geraniums. She glanced up as he passed, halted her pruning, and came over to him.

"Did you find Mayor Frey?" she asked.

"Harriet Tilson of the Parasol Ladies Association," Fargo said and she nodded with a smile.

"You never did say your name," Harriet Tilson reminded him.

"Skye Fargo," he said. "And I found the mayor, not that he helped any." He paused, studied the woman for a moment. "Maybe you're the one to help. I've been called here to find out what happened to Doc Emerson. Maybe you saw him the day he disappeared."

"No, I'm afraid not," the woman said.

"Maybe some of the other ladies of the town saw

him that day. I'd be obliged if you could ask them," Fargo said.

"I suppose I could do that," Harriet Tilson said. "Stop by in a day or two. I'll tell you what I've found out."

"I'd appreciate it," Fargo said, and Harriet Tilson offered a polite smile.

"Who called you here to ask about Doc's disappearance? I understood it was simply an unfortunate tragedy," she said.

"Emily Holden."

"I see. How unkind of her."

"Unkind?"

"Yes. She's implying it was something more than a terrible accident when the entire town has been most good to her and Doc Emerson," the woman said, her voice growing coolly disapproving.

"I think she just wants to make sure it wasn't anything more than an accident," Fargo said.

"I think she just refuses to accept reality," Harriet Tilson said, moved away, and returned to her pruning with the kind of concentration that ended any further conversation.

Fargo rode the Ovaro from town. Harriet Tilson had been the only one who had offered any kind of cooperation, and he thought of her words about Emily refusing to accept reality. They were words he couldn't dismiss, but before he rode out of sight of Parasol, he halted and looked back at the town. Doc Emerson had been one of the most well-known figures in town, yet absolutely no one remembered seeing him on the day he vanished. More than a little hard to believe, Fargo thought, and the obvious resentment at his questions stayed with him. Not that he'd make any conclusions yet. Many towns resented outsiders coming in, especially with disturbing questions. Yet in some instances he had detected more than resentment. He'd picked up a furtiveness, almost a fear. It was all a little strange and he wasn't through asking questions.

However, he had to wait for nightfall. He turned into the low hills as the sun began to edge behind the high peaks. He found a spot under a red ash, dismounted, and stretched out on a mat of rose moss. He'd let the night throw its blanket deeply before he returned to town. The dance hall would be open and in full swing by then. It was the same in every town. The dance hall was a place where men's tongues loosened and gossip found respectability. Perhaps he'd get answers he'd not been able to find anywhere else so far. He closed his eyes, pushed aside further speculation, and let himself nap. He woke often and returned to napping until he rose, finally, when the moon hung high in the black velvet sky.

He rode back to Parasol, the neat houses on the outskirts of town mostly shuttered, the main street dark and silent, until he came to the dance hall, where the murmur of laughter and voices rode the shaft of light into the street. He tethered the pinto and noted that the other mounts were mostly short-legged mountain horses. He pushed the double doors open and took in the large room with one searching glance. It was typical, little different from hundreds of others he had seen—a bar along one wall, perhaps a dozen round tables circling a small open dancing area where no one danced. A dozen men lounged at the bar, and Fargo saw six girls in too-tight dresses moving around the room with more boredom than interest. A large woman with tight, brassy curls over a puffy face filled a harsh-green dress to overflowing. Fargo made his way across the room toward her.

"Hello, stranger," she said when he reached her, taking in his powerful frame and chiseled handsomeness with a practiced eye. "I'd guess you're looking for something special, big man," she said.

"I am." Fargo nodded. "I didn't get your name, honey."

"Dolores Bantry," the madam said with a touch of surprise.

Fargo smiled. Very few of her customers ever asked her name, he was certain. "I want some information, Dolores. I'll pay for it," he said. "Talk instead of tits."

The madam folded her puffy face into a frown. "What kind of information?"

"About Doc Emerson," Fargo said. "You knew him? Any of your girls knew him?"

"Yes, we knew him."

"Then he treated you or some of your girls."

"Sometimes. He sure wasn't a customer."

"You hear anything about his sudden disappearance?" Fargo asked. The veil of caution slid across the woman's face. It was a veil he'd grown accustomed to seeing in Parasol.

"No," she said.

"Maybe some of your girls heard something."

"They didn't hear anything," the woman said with sudden firmness.

"How do you know? They tell you everything they hear?"

"That's right," Dolores said, meeting his eyes with a defiant stare.

"Mind if I ask them myself?"

"Yes, I mind. I don't want them bothered. They get upset easy."

Fargo's glance roved over the six girls with their

bored, hard-bitten, jaded faces. "I can see they're real sensitive."

"They are," the madam snapped. "Anything else?"

"Guess not," Fargo said, and moved across the room to the bartender, a man whose hard, unsmiling face had none of the agreeable openness that was the mark of most bartenders.

"What'll you have?" the man almost growled.

"Bourbon and some information," Fargo said pleasantly.

"You can get the bourbon," the bartender said as he poured the shot glass and started to turn away.

"You haven't heard what kind of information I want, friend," Fargo said.

"I know what you're after," the bartender growled.

"How do you know?" Fargo pressed.

"You hear about everything from behind a bar," the man said.

"Exactly why I stopped by," Fargo said. "Any of your customers say anything about Doc Emerson to you?"

"Nobody said anything," the barkeep muttered.

"You hear everything. You heard about me. But you haven't heard a word about Doc Emerson's disappearance. Kind of hard to believe," Fargo said.

"That's what the man said," a deep voice interrupted, and Fargo turned to see a figure that looked more like a small house than a man. At least six feet two inches and over three hundred pounds, Fargo guessed, the huge man wore a gray shirt with great gaps between each button, and trousers that barely went around legs as thick as young oak trees. He had a heavy paunch and a layer of fat all over, but there was weight and power with the fat, Fargo knew. The man's shoulders went into his head with only the vestige of a neck in between, and his face was made of overlapping jowls and eyes that glittered out of fleshy folds. Trouble, Fargo muttered as he turned to face the man's huge bulk.

"I don't believe I was talking to you, cousin," Fargo said evenly.

"I don't like the way you were talking to my friend," the man rumbled.

"I'm sorry about that," Fargo said placatingly, unwilling to play into the man's hands.

"You're nosy. I don't like nosy people," the hulk muttered, and again Fargo kept his voice calm.

"That's your right," he said.

"You know what I do to nosy people?" the huge man asked.

"Tell me," Fargo said.

"I fix them so's they don't ask any more questions," the hulk said.

The man wasn't about to be turned aside, Fargo decided. He had come on purpose. Or had been sent. But he'd try to draw the huge man out more.

"You afraid of questions about Doc Emerson?" he asked.

The double-jowled face darkened. "Me afraid? You joking, mister?" the man said.

"Who is, then?" Fargo tossed back. "Who sent you?"

The fleshy face darkened further. "I told you, you ask too many questions," the man thundered, and took a lumbering step forward.

Fargo, his back still against the bar, began to move his hand toward the Colt at his side when he felt the unmistakable pressure of the end of a rifle barrel in his back.

"Don't move, mister," he heard the bartender growl,

the rifle pressing harder against his back. "He's not carryin' a gun."

"I just want to keep him where he is," Fargo said as he felt the bartender's hand reach over the bar and pull the Colt from its holster. The rifle in his back drew away and Fargo cast a quick glance at the bartender as the man stepped back.

"Now it'll be a fair fight," the barkeep said with a grin of sneering anticipation.

"You've a damn funny idea of fair," Fargo muttered, and turned his eyes to the huge form that moved toward him, arms swinging loosely. This would be no fair fight, Fargo thought. It was never intended as such. It was intended to maim, maybe murder, all disguised as a barroom brawl. He'd meet it on those terms.

3

The hulking shape continued to come at him and Fargo saw the deadly anticipation in the glittering eyes. He moved away from the bar and let himself lift onto the balls of his feet as he watched the long, swinging arms. He saw the man's huge hands tighten, and he was ready for the first blow, a long, looping swing that was faster than he'd expected, though he easily pulled away from it. Another follow-up blow again surprised him by its speed, and in a half-crouch, Fargo shot a left out, sank it into the man's midsection. His fist disappeared in the paunch and the man only grunted as he continued to come forward.

The others in the dance hall had drawn back and now lined the walls, Fargo saw, except for the bartender, who looked on from behind the bar. The Trailsman pulled away from another series of wildly swinging punches, letting the huge figure snarl and rush at him again. He stayed in place, ducked low, and drove upward with a powerful, short left and a right that followed instantly. Both blows would have sent the ordinary man down. The huge figure's head snapped upward for an instant and the little eyes blinked, but then he charged forward again with a snarl of rage.

Fargo pulled away from another flurry of lunging blows, parried two, and felt the weight and force of the man against his forearms. Suddenly the mountainous shape slowed his lunges and came forward with almost dancing steps, and Fargo backed away, lashed out with two lightninglike blows that brought a stream of blood from the side of the fleshy face. The hulk roared in fury at once and charged again. Fargo backtracked, avoided the first lunge, then the second, and found himself near the round-topped tables.

His opponent rushed again, swinging with both arms. Fargo ducked and brought up a short left hook that landed on the heavy jaw. The hulk paused, shook his head, and sent a shower of blood into the air. He charged again and Fargo waited, measured off split seconds, and then ducked aside as the huge bulk brushed past him not unlike a buffalo in full charge. Skye stuck out one foot and tripped the onrushing figure, and one of the tables smashed to the floor as the mountainous man crashed atop it. The hulking figure quickly pushed to one knee half atop the table and Fargo stepped in and slammed a kick hard into the man's ribs. Again, the hulk grunted, but there was pain in the sound as he fell sideways. The man pushed to his feet again and Fargo saw the hate in his glittering eyes.

The man reached down, picked up the round tabletop, and held it in front of him as he came forward with slow steps first, then another charge with the tabletop held shieldlike in front of his body. Fargo swore as he backed. There was no way he could get a punch in without smashing his hands against the tabletop. He tried two straight left jabs, but the giant lifted the edge of the table and Fargo pulled his punches back. Once again, with a roar, the huge figure came at him, the tabletop held in front of him. Fargo counted off seconds once more. The giant would charge past him if he timed it right, carried on by his own momentum, Fargo calculated. It would give him time and chance to smash a blow into the man's spine with all his strength. Fargo moved backward, letting the huge figure build up more of his headlong charge. When the man was almost atop him, ready to smash the tabletop into him, Fargo twisted aside while he kept his balance, ready to whirl back and deliver his counterblow.

But the huge figure, without halting his charge, flung the tabletop sideways as though rolling a wagon wheel in midair. Fargo, twisted away, could only see the tabletop crash into him, and felt the jarring pain as he went sprawling. He hit the floor with the tabletop half over him, winced, and began to push his way out from under it. He glimpsed the huge form come down over him. He swung a right, an awkward blow from an awkward position, and the man's arm swept it aside with a kind of brutal contempt. He tried to roll but felt the huge arms around him, felt himself lifted as though he were a child. He managed to smash his elbow into the side of the man's face before he went sailing through the air. The pain exploded in his ribs as he slammed into the edge of a table and somersaulted backward with it as it crashed to the floor. He tried to push to his feet, but the huge form fell over him and he heard his own gasp of pain as the man's knee smashed into the small of his back.

The knee lifted from his back and huge arms encircled his neck. Fargo felt his breath being constricted at once as he was dragged backward. The encircling forearms tightened and Fargo heard his own breath quickly become a wheezing gasp. With frightening quickness, the weakness began to sweep over him as his life's breath began to drain from him. He brought both hands up, closed them around the thick forearms, and tried to pull them loose, only to quickly realize it was an impossibility.

Drawing on the desperate strength of those who see death becoming an imminent reality, Fargo gathered his powerful leg muscles and kicked back and up with all the strength remaining in him. His foe let out a guttural bellow of pain as the kick smashed upward into his genitals. His viselike grip loosened for only an instant, but it was enough for Fargo to tear himself away. He fell forward over one of the smashed tables and fell to his knees, drawing in deep gasps of breath.

The huge man, one hand clutching his genitals, rose from one knee and flung himself forward with a roar of fury and pain. Fargo managed a looping right that landed on the man's chin but without enough strength behind it to stop the driving hulk. Again, the mountainous figure smashed into him, and the back of his head struck the edge of one of the tables. The world exploded in flashing red and yellow lights. He managed to roll, shake his head, and the flashing lights blinked off long enough for him to see the sledgehammer fist come down on the back of his neck. He pitched forward as the waves of pain shot downward, consuming his body. Only his own strength kept him from passing out. The room spun, grew hazy, and again he shook his head to clear it. He glimpsed the massive arm descending, really only the shadow of it, and managed to twist himself to one side as the blow smashed into the table.

Fargo rolled and heard the splintering of wood as the table shattered. He shook away the haze that kept trying to descend over his eyes. He wanted to reach down to the throwing knife inside the calf holster he wore, but once again his assailant gave him no time, charging at him not unlike a wounded buffalo. Fargo rolled on the floor and cried out at the wave of pain that coursed through his body. The hulk shifted his charge, reached his treelike arms out, seeking to clasp Fargo's throat again. But the Trailsman flung himself forward and flat this time, smashing into the man's ankles, and felt the huge figure fall forward, his hands grasping only air. Fargo twisted, snakelike, along the floor and saw the broken table leg only inches from his hand. He reached out, seized the table leg, and rolled half onto one knee as the hulking figure lunged at him again.

Holding the splintered end of the table leg forward, Fargo drove the makeshift weapon into the fleshy face with all his remaining strength. The jarring force of the blow sent shock waves of pain through his own body, but he saw the man's face disappear in a fountain of red. The hulking shape halted, staggered backward, and roared in pain as blood showered from his open mouth. Fargo drew the table leg back again, swung it in a wide, horizontal arc this time, and smashed it into the man's throat just beneath his hanging jaw. He heard the shattering sounds of the tiny bones of the trachea, and the man's blood-spattered roar became a succession of hoarse, gasped sounds. He brought his hands to his throat as he staggered and collapsed into a heap.

Fargo let the table leg hang from his hand as he felt the pain that coursed through his own body. He turned slowly, moved toward the bar, his lake-blue eyes cold as January ice. Slowly, he lifted the bloodied end of the table leg and pointed it at the bartender as he advanced. "My gun, you bastard," Fargo growled. "One wrong move and you'll be as dead as he is."

The barkeep, fear in his eyes now, carefully brought the Colt from under the bar and slid it across the top. "I just wanted to see a fair fight," he stammered.

"Sure you did," Fargo said as he let the table leg fall from his hand and picked up the Colt. He turned slowly, the Colt raised in his hand. Some of the mountain men showed an open fear, the kind that said they were afraid of what he might do next. But the madam and a few others held another kind of fear in their faces—the closed, inward fear of those afraid of what hadn't happened. As the pain shot through his body, most severe at the base of his neck, he made his way across the room, aware of the silent stares that followed him. He stumbled from the dance hall into the night outside. He paused at the Ovaro and leaned against the horse as he fought off nausea and dizziness. With a groan of agony, he pulled himself into the saddle and turned the horse up the silent street.

He kept the horse at a walk as he fought off successive waves of pain and weakness. The trip seemed endless, the night a void of constant pain, and he clung to the saddle horn with both hands. Somehow, he found Twin Table Rock, or perhaps the Ovaro found it on his own, he realized, and he rode forward, wincing with the horse's every step. But Doc Emerson's house finally came in sight, a lamp lighted in one window. The Ovaro halted in front of the door and Fargo swung one leg over the saddle. A burst of pain spread down his back like a searing flame. The night faded away and he knew he was falling. He heard more than felt the dull thud as he hit the ground and the world ceased to exist.

Softness. Warmth. Soothing.

The feelings drifted into his conscious mind, hung

there lazily. Slowly, Fargo pulled his eyes open and saw only blurriness first, then colors, vision growing clearer, rearranging vagueness into shapes. He saw short brown hair, a pleasant face, a near form in a blue robe leaning over him. He blinked and the face became Emily Holden. He lifted his head enough to see that he was naked except for his drawers. Emily's hands were moving along his ribs, gently rubbing. He saw a short, wide bottle on the nearby bedside table.

"Hello," Emily said.

Fargo winced as he moved, his ribs stabbing a sharp pain into him. "You drag me in here all by yourself?" he asked.

"It wasn't easy," Emily admitted with a wry smile. "I heard you fall." Her fingers continued to gently massage his ribs, and he felt the cool salve she was rubbing in.

"That feels good," he murmured.

"Balm of Gilead, birch bark, white-willow bark compress, wintergreen compress, hyssop, and lily root, all mixed with a witch hazel base. Greatest ointment for bruises and muscle strains," Emily said. He moved his back and the pain that had been so agonizing was only a dull echo of its former self. "You received a blow on your neck that spread down your entire back," Emily said.

"I received a blow, all right."

"You want to tell me what happened?"

"From the beginning." He nodded and proceeded to recount the details of his visit to Parasol, finishing with the attack in the dance hall.

"How strange," Emily murmured when he finished, and rested her hands upon his chest. "What do you make of it?"

"I don't know, but somebody was stupid tonight," Fargo said.

"Meaning what?"

"Meaning I was bothered by the way folks answered me. Meaning I probably would've just stayed bothered if I got nothing more than that. I've seen other towns that didn't like strangers snooping into their affairs. People's answers don't make a crime. But tonight I got something more. Somebody was afraid enough to have me killed in a barroom brawl."

"Now you know I was right. I wasn't just being suspicious. Doc Emerson's disappearance was no accident," Emily said, excitement in her voice.

"Whoa, now, not so fast," Fargo said. "I'm convinced something's wrong, but that's all so far. I'm not saying it's what you're thinking."

"You said everybody seemed afraid to even talk about Doc Emerson's disappearance, except to call me names."

"People can be afraid for all kinds of reasons. They can be afraid because they're hiding something, or they can be afraid for their own lives. They can be afraid because they don't want to get involved in something or because they're trying to protect someone. It doesn't have to be what you're thinking."

"A whole town afraid. I can't accept that," Emily said.

"Accept it. I've seen it happen," Fargo said. "There's something here, I'll give you that. But it might not be as simple as you see it."

She fixed him with a thoughtful gaze. "You've something you're not saying," Emily murmured.

He smiled at her quickness. "Nothing with shape to it," he said, and started to push up on his elbows, wincing at the pain that immediately shot through his body. He fell back at once and Emily took more of the salve and rubbed it on his sides, gently drawing her fingers along his shoulders and muscled arms. He watched her eyes take in the powerful symmetry of his body. She finished, dried her hands on a small towel she had on the table, and met his eyes with a properly professional glance.

"Get a good sleep. Sleep late in the morning. Your body needs it," she said.

"Thanks for everything, especially the massaging and the ointment. You're real good," Fargo observed.

"I'm a nurse," she said, keeping her face proper.

"I'm glad. I wouldn't want you enjoying it."

"Good night," she said, rising at once and hurrying from the room, pulling the door shut after her.

He winced again as he reached over and turned out the lamp and the blackness flowed over him. Thoughts drifted slowly through his mind. It had been a day of unsatisfactory answers and a night that brought more questions, but he was too drained to wrestle with all the shadowy possibilities. His body cried out for sleep and he closed his eyes and let the demands of exhaustion sweep everything else away. He slept deeply and, his own inner clock set, woke when the new day broke over the peaks.

He rose and stretched. His back still ached, but the sharp, stabbing pain was gone and his ribs were throbbing dully. He dressed and washed quickly, taking extra care to be silent. When he finally left the room, he saw the door ajar to Emily's room. He paused, peered in to see her asleep, one bare leg out from beneath the sheet, slender yet nicely shaped. He hurried from the house and went to the stable, saddled the Ovaro, and led the horse across the front yard, swinging into the saddle only when he was a dozen yards from the house. He put the horse into a canter, rode down the road, and finally turned into the mountains. The morning mists were still heavy, a succession of wispy, carelessly thrown scarves that circled the hills as he rode to the spot where he had first seen the black-clad horseman.

The morning mists still swirled when he reached the deep hollow surrounded by the four hills. He edged the Ovaro forward slowly through thick growths of hawthorn and peered into the last wisps of the mist. He brought his eyes up to the nearest mountainside and came to a halt as he saw the lone rider moving along the narrow, winding trail. Wearing a tan shirt with a ten-gallon hat pulled low over his face, he rode the same trail the other man had taken two mornings ago. No, Fargo muttered, correcting himself quickly. The man rode a deer trail a dozen yards higher and to the left.

Fargo's eyes swung from the lone rider as he caught the movement in the blue spruce halfway down the hill and he saw the black-clad rider emerge from the heavy tree cover. The rider moved quickly, rifle raised to fire. The shot came at once, reverberating through the deep hollow. Fargo flicked a glance at the rider on the deer trail and saw the man toss his arms into the air and topple from his horse.

Fargo tore his eyes from the figure in time to see the black-clad horseman already racing into the spruce at the bottom of the hollow. The Trailsman sent the pinto racing down the side of the hill as he cursed the treacherous steepness that made even the surefooted Ovaro slip and slide. The rider in black had already vanished into the trees when Fargo reached the bottom of the hill, but he quickly spotted the bruised shrubs where the horseman had ridden into the spruce. Skye followed the trail, pushing as fast as the tangled and dense terrain would permit. The fleeing figure raced in the same direction he had the last time, Fargo noted, and he suddenly reined up sharply as he came to the steep side of the hill he had faced during his last pursuit. He stared at the ground where the horse's prints halted at a section of wide, flat rock in front of the steep hill.

Fargo moved the Ovaro to his right, recrossed to search to the left, but there were no other hoofprints. He returned to the set of prints in front of the high, almost straight hillside of flat rock and brush-covered soil. Once again, the black-clad rider had seemingly vanished into thin air at the same spot he had last time.

Fargo swung to the ground and walked to the almost straight hillside, letting his eyes roam over the tall sections of flat rock that rose high up on the steep sides. He moved to the left and peered at the brush-covered, almost perpendicular hillside of soil. Once again, he saw that only pine squirrels or martens could climb that steep side. He turned away and carefully examined the earth on both sides of where he stood, dropping to one knee to feel the grass. Sometimes the hand could find indentations the eye failed to see. But there were no hoofprints, and he rose with a grimace.

It was the same place, the hackberry heavy on all sides, the side of rock and earth unlike any other nearby. The same place, no mistaking it, he grunted. "Damn it to hell. Either he can really vanish into thin air or he's the best damn rider I've ever followed," Fargo swore, and was instantly unwilling to accept either explanation. Yet the figure in black had given him no other choice, he realized angrily. He climbed onto the pinto and sent the horse at a trot through the hackberry and into the spruce. When he emerged from the spruce, he turned to the adjoining mountain slope and climbed its steepness to the highest of the deer trails. When he reached it, he stared at the place where he'd seen the man topple from his horse, and once again there was no slain form. Flinging an oath into the air, he dropped to the ground and searched the brush and trees alongside the deer trail. But exactly as the last time, there were no drops of blood on the ground, no signs of a figure that had dragged itself into the brush. Again, the rifleman and the victim had vanished.

But this time Fargo did see hoofprints going down the deer trail. Had the man managed to pull himself onto his horse and leave? Fargo followed on foot, the Ovaro moving along behind him. His eyes peering at the ground, he sought telltale drops of blood but found none. The hoofprints showed the horse moving steadily, with no pauses or slowing, as a wounded rider might do. Halfway down the slope, the deer trail faded away into a thick forest of Rocky Mountain maple and the heavy leaf cover on the ground made further tracking impossible.

Fargo backed the Ovaro onto the deer trail again and rode upward this time until he found a place where he could cross onto the other slope. He climbed up to the top of the mountainside and left the hollow with a last backward glance of angry frustration.

The morning sun was high when he arrived back at Doc Emerson's house and saw Emily come to the open door, her slender, neat figure clothed in a dark-brown dress that buttoned down the front yet fitted tight enough to outline the nice shape of her modest breasts. He dismounted and met her angry frown.

"Where have you been? Dammit, Fargo, I told you to sleep late," she snapped.

"I know what you said, honey."

"You needed the extra sleep. You were very battered last night."

"That sounds like real concern." Fargo smiled and she instantly wrapped her face in coolness, but he saw the two tiny spots of color touch her cheeks.

"I'm a nurse. I'm always concerned about my patients."

"I bounce back quickly." Fargo grinned and drew a glare of disapproval. "I went back to that hollow in the mountains. I wanted to be there in the early morning again."

"Did you find anything?" Emily asked skeptically.

"I sure as hell did," Fargo said, and saw the skepticism sweep from her face. "No morning mists playing tricks, not the first time and not this time," he said, and quickly recounted what he had seen. "The same damn thing," he said when he finished. "The damn rider in black disappears, and so do his victims. I'm guessing he works with someone. He does the shooting and somebody else gets rid of his victims. But I can't figure out how the hell he disappears into thin air."

"And you think this has something to do with Doc Emerson's disappearance?" Emily asked.

"It could be the answer. What if this killer came on to Doc Emerson in the mountains and killed him just as he did the two men I saw him kill?"

"What reason would he have to kill Doc?"

"Some killers don't need a reason," Fargo said. "Maybe the doc saw something he shouldn't have. That'd be reason enough."

Emily's smooth brow stayed furrowed as she considered his words. "But why would the whole town be afraid? Why would somebody be sent after you?"

"Maybe this black-clad rider has some connection

with the town. I've seen whole towns afraid of one man with power and ruthlessness," Fargo said.

"The only people I know of in town with power are the mayor and Myron Beezer, but you said they seemed afraid, too," Emily countered. "No, I can't go along with you on this connection."

"All I said was maybe. I don't know more than that," Fargo said. "But I aim to find out."

"That's all I want," Emily said, her face relaxing. "I've still got the coffeepot on."

"Now, that sounds good." Fargo nodded and followed her into the house, her firm rear moving with a neatness that just avoided a sway.

She poured coffee for them both and looked at him over the rim of her mug. "What next?" she asked with the directness that was part of her.

"I pay another visit to town. You said the doc had an office there. Did you look through it since he disappeared?"

"I just looked at his date pad. There's not much else there."

"Come with me. Maybe he kept files that might tell us something."

"We can look, but I doubt we'll find anything much. Doc was never big on paperwork and files," Emily said, and took his empty mug into the kitchen.

Fargo heard the sound of a wagon rolling to a halt outside. He stepped to the door with her to see an elderly man in a battered buckboard.

"It's Jake Azard," Emily said.

"It's Celia. A real bad attack this time," the man called.

"I'll be right along, Jake," Emily said, and turned to Fargo.

"You seem to know what it is," he said.

"Yes, it's Jake's daughter. She's a young woman—not over thirty, I'd guess. But she has some kind of lung condition that gives her terrible attacks. Doc used to treat her regularly," Emily said. "I've been sort of holding the fort as best I can until the town finds a new doc. I've got to go with him."

"All right, we can visit the office tonight," Fargo said as Emily picked up a small black bag and started for the door. He halted her for a moment, an arm blocking her way. "You go on any more calls when I'm not here, you leave a note telling me where," he said.

"All right. Jake Azard's place is three miles past town in the foothills. I'll be back by night," Emily said.

"I'll come by for you," Fargo said, and watched her drive away in the buckboard with Jake Azard. He went outside, climbed onto the Ovaro, and rode slowly to town. He drew up to a neat house at the outskirts.

Harriet Tilson came out, a wide apron over a yellow dress. "Fargo, I'm glad you came by. I was just about to go meet Carrie Hamilton. We're going blackberry picking," the woman explained. "I did speak to a number of the ladies in the association. None of them saw Doc Emerson that day. I'm sorry."

"Thanks for asking," Fargo said, and Harriet Tilson gave him a smile edged with patient tolerance.

"We were all saying how sorry we feel for Emily," she said. "I'm afraid she's brought you into her own reluctance to face facts. I hope you won't waste too much of your own time on Emily's delusions. Just a suggestion, of course," she added with another patient smile.

"I'll keep that in mind," Fargo said as he moved on into town. He rode slowly, his eyes again taking in

56

Parasol, watching the men and women who were obviously townspeople, and the mountain men who were merely passing through. Scanning the neat shops and the well-kept houses, he saw a sign outside the Town Meeting Hall he hadn't noticed before. *Sunday Church Service—11 o'clock*, it read, and he felt a nagging sense of something wrong as he rode on. It stayed there and he didn't know why. He had reached the bank when he saw Myron Beezer hurrying toward him in his gray frock coat.

"Fargo . . . hold on there," the banker called out. "We were just talking about you. Mayor Frey's inside. I know he wants to see you. Come inside with me."

Fargo dismounted and followed the banker inside, where the man led him to the inner office. A small room, Fargo noted, with a desk, two stuffed chairs, and a heavy iron safe against one wall. The mayor rose from one of the chairs as he entered, a moment of surprise in his sharp face.

"Just saw Mr. Fargo riding by, Harold," the banker said, and Mayor Frey nodded and let a smile soften his face, though his eyes remained cold and probing.

"Myron and I both want to say how sorry we are for that terrible attack on you last night at the dance hall," the mayor said. "Parasol's a small town. News travels fast."

"Some of these mountain men who come to town are plain wild and mean," the banker put in. "They'll use any excuse for a fight."

"This one seemed to be mad over my asking questions about Doc Emerson," Fargo said mildly.

"Nonsense. As Myron said, they'll use any excuse," the mayor answered quickly. "But we feel we ought to warn you. A lot of these back-mountain people resent strangers and resent being asked questions. I think you'd best be discreet with your questions."

"Not only back-mountain people. A lot of folks here in town have been brushing me off," Fargo said.

"No, no, don't think that. There's a difference between having nothing to say and being resentful," the banker offered.

"So there is," Fargo agreed. "And there's a difference between being honest and being afraid."

A flash of harshness swept over the mayor's face for an instant, and his smile took an extra moment to form, Fargo noted. "I guess what Myron and I are trying to say is that we hope you've concluded there's nothing more to be found out about poor Doc Emerson's disappearance than we already know," the man said.

"I've concluded I'm not through looking around," Fargo said, and saw Harold Frey keep his pleasant smile with an effort as the corners of his mouth twitched.

"Of course, you just go on. We want you and Emily to be satisfied," Myron Beezer put in quickly. "You just call on us if there's any way we can help."

"Count on it." Fargo nodded pleasantly and turned to leave. As he did so, he glanced again at the short, squat iron safe in Myron Beezer's inner office and wondered idly what he kept in there that he couldn't keep in the big outside safe. He strolled past Lucille Todman at her desk; he smiled at her and received a polite nod in return.

Outside, Fargo returned to the pinto and continued his slow stroll through town. As he reached the general store, he saw Ben Stoppard turn away as he passed, his face sullen. Sam the barber stared at him from inside his shop as he rode by. Fargo saw Tom Riley halt his hammering on a boot to watch him ride on. The good citizens of Parasol seemed more than resentful, Fargo mused. They seemed hostile—almost too much so, even for a town resentful of strangers.

He reached the end of town, halted, and turned the Ovaro to gaze back along the main street. Parasol stretched out before him, the neat buildings, the feeling of solidity, the proper stores for a proper town, its mixture of townspeople and those just passing through. A proper and respectable town, it was, and yet there was something wrong. He couldn't give it shape, but it was there. Something wrong. Or perhaps more accurately, something not right, he thought as he peered at the town. But the shape of it eluded him and he turned the horse around and pushed the thought from his mind for the moment, aware that to try to force the undefined into shape never worked. He'd return to his unformed thought again, he knew.

He put the Ovaro into a canter and rode into the low hills. He followed a path that led through a stand of red oak and slowly wound itself higher into the low hills. He was eager to explore the other part of these mountains. He had ridden for more than an hour in his circuitous path when he heard voices from just beyond a thick cluster of mountain brush directly ahead of him.

A man's voice came to him first, then a young woman's voice and then another man with a high-pitched laugh. He moved the Ovaro forward slowly and silently. A clearing came into sight and he saw the water of a spring-fed mountain pond. The young woman's head and shoulders were over the surface of the clear blue pond as she treaded water in one spot.

The two men, their horses nearby, stood at the edge of the pond. "Come on out, honey. You're gonna freeze your little ass stayin' in there so long," the one said, and the other gave another high-pitched, whinnying laugh.

Fargo took in the two men with a glance, both

medium height, one with a short mustache, the other with a long, narrow nose. Drifters, he reckoned, trail packs on their horses, worn boots, and gun belts of cracked and chipped leather.

Fargo's eyes went to the girl and he saw nicely rounded shoulders, black hair that hung loosely around what seemed an attractive face upon a quick glance.

"How long have you been watching?" the young woman called out.

" 'Bout since you went in," the mustached one said.

"Then you've seen enough. Get out of here," the girl snapped.

"You're right, little lady. We've done enough lookin'. Now we aim to do some touchin'," the man said, and the other broke into his whinnying, high-pitched laugh.

"Like hell," the young woman said.

"You come out or we'll come in and get you," the one said, and stepped to where Fargo saw the young woman had placed her clothes in a neat pile. "Sooner we all finish, the sooner you can put these nice clothes back on, girlie," he said, and lifted the pile of clothes with one hand. As he did so, the six-gun fell from the center of the clothes, a big, six-shot single-action Allen and Wheelock, Fargo noted. The drifter stared down at the gun in surprise as it lay at the edge of the pond, raised his eyes to look out into the pond. "Now, what's a nice little thing like you gonna do with a big gun like that?" he asked.

"Use it on bastards like you," the young woman flung back.

"Then you should've taken it swimming with you, girlie," the man said, laughing.

"Goddammit, bitch, get out of there," the long-nosed one suddenly roared, his voice harsh.

"Now, look what you did," the first drifter said to

the young woman. "You went and got Jud mad, and now he's as like to shoot you as screw you. You come out right now afore he gets madder."

Fargo moved the Ovaro through the brush, and the two men turned at once, surprise spreading across both their faces. "Fun's over, gents. Time to move on," Fargo said quietly.

"Who the hell are you?" the one with the mustache said.

"That doesn't matter. You boys just move on and there'll be no trouble," Fargo said.

"You're not getting this for yourself, mister. We were here first. You move the hell on," the long-nosed one snarled.

" 'Less you want an early funeral," the other added.

Fargo's eyes moved from one man to the other and he let a weary sigh escape his lips. "That's real dumb talk. I don't want shooting and killing."

"That's big of you, seeing as how there are two of us and one of you, mister," one of the drifters sneered.

"Wrong reason, but that doesn't much matter, either. You boys just move on and everybody will be happy," Fargo said.

"Not you, mister. You'll be dead," the mustached one snarled, and Fargo saw the twitch of his hand a split second before he went for his gun. His gun hadn't cleared its holster when the big Colt was in Fargo's hand and firing, a single shot that caught the man full in the chest. The Trailsman had the Colt shifted at the second man, whose hand was still on his gun butt as his eyes grew wide with surprise and fear.

"No, Jesus . . . I'm not drawing," the man sputtered with a quick glance at the figure on its back on the ground.

"That shows you're smarter than he was," Fargo

commented evenly, and saw the man drop his hand to his side, fear filling his face. "Pick him up, lay him over his horse, and get out of here with him," Fargo ordered.

"Yes, sir," the drifter said, and quickly dragged his recently alive cohort to one of the horses; he flung the limp form over the saddle and hurriedly climbed onto his own horse.

"Don't come back," Fargo said. "Don't even think about it."

"No, sir. I won't be thinking about it, you can take my word for that," the drifter said, snapped the reins on his horse, and rode away with the other horse and its silent rider behind him.

Fargo holstered the Colt, swung from the Ovaro, and faced the young woman still in the water.

"Thanks," she called out. "That was the fastest draw I ever saw."

"You can come out now," Fargo said.

She frowned. "Not again," she said.

"I think I deserve some kind of reward," he remarked blandly.

"Not if you're going to be just the same as they were," she returned, and he grinned as he shrugged.

"Good enough answer for now," he agreed, and turned his back to the water and listened to the sounds of her as she came out of the pond, used a towel to dry herself, and quickly pulled on clothes.

"You can turn around now," she said, and he did so to see a full figure clothed in a tan blouse and tan skirt, full breasts that pressed the front of the blouse smooth except for two small points, and womanly hips that flared from a narrow waist. Up close, her face became more than attractive—lips that were full, a straight nose, and wide cheekbones with black hair hanging loosely with a careless kind of loveliness. But it was her eyes that held him, a penetrating gray that seemed to glow with a combination of turbulence and coolness somehow mixed together. A face of sensuality, he decided. She had tucked the big Allen and Wheelock into the waistband of her skirt, he noted.

"Exactly what did you bring that along for?' he asked, nodding to the revolver with his eyes.

"Stray Nez Percé," she said. "I didn't see any. No tracks, either. I thought I was safe enough." She paused, a tiny smile touching her eyes. "I didn't expect you'd be so good-looking," she said, and her smile widened at the surprise that came over the big man's chiseled face. "You're Fargo, the one who's been asking about Doc Emerson," she said.

"You live in Parasol?" Fargo asked.

"No, but I was there yesterday for some supplies. I heard talk. That Ovaro of yours was mentioned. I'm Sibyl Danner. I live with my father and brother in Apple Valley. That's around the other side of the mountain."

"Hello, Sibyl," Fargo said, smiling.

"Hello, Fargo." The young woman laughed, a low, husky sound. "I owe you. How about we start with a good supper at my place? I'd like Pa and Matt to meet you."

"Sounds good, but I'll have to skip supper. Emily Holden will be waiting for me. We've some things to do," Fargo said.

"Supper can be another night. But you can meet Matt and Pa now," she said, and he watched as Sibyl Danner brought her horse from behind a tall slab of rock. She swung into the saddle with an easy, fluid motion, breasts swaying in unison and the loose black hair tossing to one side. There was a sensual quality to her every movement, he decided, a feeling of emotions without constraint, not unlike a simmering volcano.

He climbed onto the pinto and rode alongside her as she led the way along the bottom of the mountainside. Perhaps Sibyl Danner would provide answers to some of the questions lurking inside him. Perhaps she'd help him understand Parasol.

"What's an uncommonly attractive young woman such as yourself do out here?" Fargo asked.

"Right now I'm helping take care of my pa," Sibyl said. "I expect I might be moving on in time." She paused and tossed him a sidelong glance with quiet laughter in her penetrating gray eyes. "Unless Parasol suddenly gets a lot more visitors such as you," she said.

"It might. You never know. Is your pa sick?"

"He was injured in an accident. He still needs looking after," Sibyl said. "My brother, Matt, takes care of bringing in eating money."

"How?"

"We buy and sell horses, just a few, nothing big, but enough to keep us going," Sibyl said.

She rode her horse easily, Fargo noted, breasts swaying gently under her shirt, her body moving gracefully with the horse and that simmering quality a part of every movement, every gesture, every glance of her gray eyes. "You knew Doc Emerson?" he asked.

"Sure. He used to come treat Pa when the pain got too bad."

"You know if he had any enemies in town?"

"None I ever heard about," Sibyl said. "Truth is, Fargo, I go along with what everyone says. There are cuts and ravines in these mountains a man can fall into and never be found, except by accident."

"Tell me about Parasol. It's a right proper town," Fargo said.

"It is," Sibyl agreed.

"So why does everybody close up like a clam when I ask about Doc Emerson?" he slid out.

"I guess folks don't want to talk about it. Maybe, in a crazy way, they feel a kind of blame for it, like they should've looked out for him more."

Fargo's lips pursed in thought. It was an explanation he hadn't considered. Plausible in its own strange way. But the attack in the dance hall flashed through his mind and he discarded the suggestion. "I keep thinking there's something more," he told Sibyl.

"I wouldn't know. We don't have much to do with town. Matt goes in for an occasional night of drinking and whoring, and Pa shows at some of the town meetings. Otherwise, we stay pretty much to ourselves," she answered. She turned under an arched bank of red ash, rounded a curve, and a narrow, flat stretch of land unfolded in front of him, a valley only because the mountains rose on both sides. He saw the house sitting alone almost in the center of the flat stretch of land, a barn nearby and a corral with half-a-dozen horses inside, all distinguished by their ordinariness.

A young man appeared as Fargo rode up to the small, compact house with Sibyl. He was younger than she, not more than twenty years old, he guessed. Fargo saw light-brown hair in a square face that held suspicion in it. "My brother, Matt," Sibyl introduced as Fargo swung to the ground and saw a figure roll out of the house in a wheelchair. The man, heavyset, in trousers and undershirt, had a beefy, florid face with a flattened nose. His thick arms maneuvered the wheelchair as though it were an almost weightless toy. "My pa, Mort Danner," Sibyl said, and quickly told both men what had happened at the pond.

"We're beholden to you, Fargo," Mort Danner said.

He reached under the wheelchair and pulled out a bottle of whiskey, took a healthy draw of it, and offered it to Fargo.

"Next time," Fargo said. "I've a lot of riding to do tonight." The man shrugged, took another drink from the bottle and pushed it under the wheelchair. Fargo saw that a small sack hung between the wheels. Mort Danner's florid face quickly became more understandable. It wasn't just from the exertion of maneuvering the wheelchair. With a nod, the man wheeled himself back into the house and Matt Danner followed.

Sibyl motioned to Fargo, led him around to one side of the house and through a side entrance. He found himself in a modest-sized room, a double bed against one wall covered with a pink sheet, and pink curtain with ruffles on the two windows, a definitely feminine room.

"How long will you be staying around, Fargo?" Sibyl asked as she leaned against a low white dresser. She leaned back against her opened palms, and the blouse pulled tight against her breasts where the two small points pressed forward boldly.

"Depends on what I find," Fargo answered.

"And if you don't find anything?"

"I'll be on my way. But that won't happen tomorrow," he said.

"Don't let Emily Holden lead you on a wild-goose chase," Sibyl said.

"You another one who thinks she's come unhinged by Doc's disappearance?" he asked.

"I wouldn't say that. I just think she's the kind who can't accept anything unfinished. I've met her type before. They want every i dotted and every t crossed. Everything has to be neat, everything in place and thoroughly explained. They can never accept that life's not like that. Life's full of hanging threads."

He smiled. Sibyl's evaluation of Emily could be entirely accurate, he realized. "There are some other things around here I'd like explained," he said, and told her of the black-clad rider who disappeared along with his victims.

Her penetrating gray eyes peered hard at him when he finished, her lovely, full lips parted. "You really expect me to believe that wild story?"

"I do and I don't, seeing as how I've trouble believing it myself," Fargo said grimly. "Only it's true."

She fixed him with a skeptical stare. "Pa's a heavy-drinking man, but then you've already noticed that," she said, and his shrug was an admission. "After a heavy bout with the bottle he talks about things he swears he's seen, only they never really happened. But he swears they did. They've become real to him."

"No dice, honey. I was sober the first time and sober the second," Fargo snapped.

"Then I sure can't explain it."

"You've never seen a rider in black roaming the mountains?"

"Never. Besides, whatever happened to Doc Emerson may have nothing to do with this mysterious rider," she said.

"It may not. Then again it may."

Sibyl shrugged. "I suppose that's so," she said almost airily. "It seems to me you've enough to do to find out about Doc Emerson without chasing down strange riders in black."

"You're probably right," Fargo agreed. "And I'd best be going now."

"When will you be back for that supper?"

"How about tomorrow night?"

"Fine," she said, took a sudden step forward, and her lips were on his, warm and soft, holding for a moment's sweet pressure before pulling back.

"That my reward?" he asked.

"That's so you don't forget to show up," Sibyl said, and walked outside with him.

Mort Danner sat in his wheelchair, the whiskey bottle in his lap. He extended a hand and Fargo felt the power in the man's grip as they shook hands.

"Anybody who does a good thing for my little girl is welcome here anytime," Mort said, and Fargo heard the slur that had come into his speech.

"Thanks." He nodded and pulled himself onto the Ovaro.

Matt Danner waved at him from the corral as Fargo rode away.

He kept the pinto at a trot as he circled the base of the high hills. It was a long-enough ride, and night had wrapped its inky arms around the land when he arrived back at Emily's, where he hurried through the open door of the house.

"Expected you back earlier," she said. "You find out anything?"

"Met someone. Sibyl Danner," he told her.

Her thin, carefully plucked eyebrows lifted. "The very desirable Sibyl Danner," she said, just a trace of waspishness in her voice.

"What's that mean?"

"It seems as though every man who meets her sets his cap for her."

"That bothers you?" Fargo asked.

"No. I'm bothered by women who toss their wares at a man. She even did it with Doc Emerson. That's how she enjoys herself. Maybe she can't help it," Emily said disdainfully.

"I got the impression she stays pretty much to herself," Fargo said.

"I think she just likes teasing," Emily said. "And

men make fools of themselves over it. I presume you'll be seeing her again."

Fargo smiled at the disapproval in her remark. "Not for the reasons you're thinking," he answered. Emily tossed him a glance of skepticism. "She's the first person around here I've met that was friendly and willing to talk. I'm hoping she'll tell me more about Parasol, maybe enough to help."

"I'm in no position to turn down anything," Emily said. "Go see her, draw her out. Just remember you're there to find out things, not enjoy yourself."

"I'll remember that, unless I can combine the two," he said, and saw the corners of Emily's lips tighten. "If I didn't know better, I'd say you were jealous of Sibyl Danner," he remarked blandly.

Emily fastened him with an icy stare. "There's a difference in not liking someone and being jealous of them," she said.

"Sometimes there is," he conceded. "And sometimes one's just wrapped inside the other."

"Are we ready to go look at Doc's office in town?" Emily snapped, ignoring his reply.

"Ladies first," he said as she strode outside to her horse.

4

Parasol was silent and dark as Fargo rode along the rear of the buildings with Emily beside him. When sound did filter through the darkness, it was the dim murmur of voices from the dance hall. "Doc's office is in the last building in town, really a small shed," Emily said, her voice a whisper.

Finally the small structure came into sight, standing alone, a dozen feet from the nearest building. When they drew closer, Fargo noticed a flicker of lamplight from the single curtained window that faced them, and he saw Emily's instant frown.

He halted only a few feet from the shed. "Stay here," he told her as he slid from the saddle, the Colt in his hand before his feet touched the ground. He was at the door in one long stride, closed one hand around the knob, and turned it silently. The door came open at once and he saw two figures inside the room. A kerosene lamp afforded them enough light as they sorted through file folders and single sheets of paper.

Fargo stepped into the room and saw both men look up in surprise. The man on the right yanked at his gun while the other one whirled and dived headlong through the window behind him to the sound of shattering glass. But the other man had his gun clear of its holster and started to bring it up. Fargo cursed as he had to fire. The man flew back across the room, to smash into the wall, but Fargo was already running to the shattered window. He gathered his powerful leg muscles, twisted his body, and flew through the window feet-first, the rest of his long frame stretched out straight.

He hit the ground outside on his feet and skidded to one knee as the man started to pull himself onto his horse. "Hold it right there or you're a dead man," Fargo shouted, and saw the man freeze in position, one hand on the saddle horn, one foot in the stirrup. The man slowly took his hand from the saddle horn and lowered his foot from the stirrup. He turned around to see the big Colt trained on him.

"Toss your gun down, real slow," Fargo said, and the man obeyed, letting the six-gun drop to the ground alongside the horse. "Walk," Fargo ordered. "Around to the front of the house." He fell in step behind the man, and when they reached the front of the building, he marched the man inside.

Emily turned as he entered behind the man and immediately stepped toward him.

"No, stay back," Fargo shouted, but he was too late. She had already come too near and the man dived and wrapped both arms around her as he spun with her. He spun her again, came up behind her, and Fargo saw a knife appear in his hand, the edge of the blade against Emily's throat.

"Drop the gun," the man rasped, and Fargo saw Emily's skin quiver as the blade pressed harder. "Hurry up, goddamn, or I cut her head off," the man snarled.

Fargo lowered the Colt and, with a quick, backhand flip, flung the gun out of the open doorway at his back.

"Bastard," the man growled, and began to move forward with Emily. "Get back," he ordered, and Fargo moved against one wall as the man slid past him, the knife still against Emily's throat. Fargo followed him out of the house. "Back off. Not so damn close," the man ordered, but Fargo continued to follow not more than a few feet away as the man backed toward his horse, Emily still in front of him.

There'd be only one opportunity, Fargo realized, if he were a good judge of human nature. The man was nearing his horse, but he'd stop to pick up his gun where he had dropped it. For a brief moment he'd have to pull the knife from against Emily's throat as he bent down for the gun. Fargo, every muscle tensed, continued to move with the man. They were almost at the gun and his eyes narrowed on the man as he halted. Moving quickly, the man bent down to pick up the pistol, the knife drawn from Emily's throat for that precious instant. Fargo leapt, all his strength in the diving spring. Emily was still in front of the man and he slammed into her just above the knees. She sailed backward, Fargo half atop her, into the figure that was still bent down retrieving the gun. All three flew into a sprawl, the man first as, still off-balance, he went down sideways. The gun skittered from his fingers.

With a backward sweep of one arm, Fargo knocked Emily to one side as he leapt onto the man. He came down hard on the man and tried to wrap one arm around his neck, but had to let go as the man lashed out in a backward blow with the knife. Fargo rolled and saw the man rising from one knee to slash again with the knife. He stayed, let the figure lunge at him and twisted away at the last split second. The man hurtled past him, the knife slicing air. Fargo stuck out his leg and the hurtling figure fell over it, stumbled, and sprawled onto the ground on his face. The Trailsman leapt after him and drove his boot hard into the small of the man's back. He expected the man to shudder and cry out in pain. Instead, he felt the man go limp and heard a soft groaning sound. He reached down and turned the man over, prepared to deliver another blow. Then he saw the hilt of the knife protruding from the figure's chest. The man's eyes stared up at him before they fluttered closed and his last breath came through his lips with a soft, hissing sound.

"Dammit," Fargo swore. "He won't be telling us anything. Not his friend, either." He straightened up and glanced at Emily. "You know him?"

"No, but I've seen the other one in town," Emily said. "He was one of those men who hung around, never doing anything much. Sometimes he'd run errands for people."

"What people?"

"Myron Beezer, all the storekeepers, anybody that paid him," she answered.

"This time somebody paid him to clean out Doc's office," Fargo said, leading the way back into the small house.

"Why, after all this time?"

"Until now there was no need to check the doc's files. But when I let it be known I was going to keep digging, it suddenly became important to get the files. You didn't think about it till now, either," Fargo reminded her.

"That's true," Emily reflected. "But this proves I was right all along: Doc Emerson didn't just disappear."

"It doesn't prove he was murdered," Fargo said.

"What else could it mean?"

"Let's say that Doc really did have an accident. But

maybe he did know something about somebody. Whatever he knew died with him. Until I came along," Fargo said.

"Then somebody got scared," Emily said, excitement rising in her voice. "Afraid Doc might have put what he'd learned into his files."

"Exactly. The first reaction was to get rid of me. That would've put an end to worrying. When that didn't work, the next move was to get Doc's files."

"Which explains their waiting till now. You suspect anyone?"

"No. Maybe it's one person. Maybe more than one," Fargo said.

"But all this doesn't explain the whole town's attitude."

"The two might not be connected. The town might just not like my poking around. Sometimes people act the same way, but for different reasons," Fargo answered, and watched Emily digest all he had said.

"I still say Doc didn't have an accident," she said after a moment.

"Maybe you're right. All I'm saying is that nothing that's happened so far proves it. Not yet, anyway. Suppose you start doing what we came here to do: go through those files."

Emily nodded and bent to the floor to pick up the scattered file papers while Fargo dragged the lifeless figure of the second man outside. Whoever sent the men would learn about their fate when they didn't return, he thought grimly, and strode back into the office.

Emily looked up from the last of the file folders. "There's nothing to help us here," she muttered. "The files carry the patient's name, a few prescriptions, some receipts for special medicines, a few visit dates, nothing else." She turned away to stare through the open door. "Two men were killed over nothing."

"It goes that way sometimes," Fargo said, and took her by the arm. "Let's get out of here." He led her to the horses.

Emily rode in silence during the trip back to her house. She had changed into a cotton nightgown that covered her completely when he returned from stabling the horses. "What next?" she asked.

"I keep looking, asking, digging," Fargo said. "Maybe I'll come onto something or maybe somebody will get more nervous and make another mistake."

"Thank you," Emily said softly, and he questioned with his eyes. "For not being discouraged," she added.

"I don't discourage easily."

"Sleep well," she said, and went into her room, her rear a small, swaying bulge under the nightgown. Somehow, she was quietly sensuous. She'd be both pleased and embarrassed by that, he was certain. Emily, he had decided, focused her directness at only one thing at a time, and it was all Doc Emerson now.

Fargo went into the other room, shed clothes, and welcomed sleep. When the dawn came, he woke, dressed quickly, and slipped softly from the room. He went to the stable and saddled the Ovaro. The morning mists still swirled when he reached the deep hollow in the mountains. He sat quietly on the horse and scanned the lush dawn landscape, letting his gaze move slowly across the deer trails on the next slope. He brought his gaze down to the land below and waited as the mists began to part, but no black-clad horseman appeared. He waited further as the morning sun burned away the last of the mists, and only the fluttered flight of grouse and the plodding pace of moose disturbed the silence of the deep hollow.

Finally, satisfied that there'd be neither black-cloaked rider nor disappearing victim, Fargo made his way from the four steep slopes and returned to the road on the other side of the mountains. He could ride the hills for a year and not find anything of Doc Emerson's, he realized. His best chance was to make something happen, to let his presence be seen in town. Somebody was already nervous, and nervousness fed on itself.

Harriet Tilson was outside pruning her bushes again when he reached Parasol; she paused to watch him go by.

Once in town, he ambled slowly down the main street and back again. When he glimpsed Mayor Frey, he halted at Sam's. "Remember anything about the day Doc Emerson disappeared?" he asked the barber casually.

"No," the man snapped, and went into his shop.

"Just like to keep asking. You never know whose memory might come back," Fargo called pleasantly, and rode on, aware of Harold Frey's eyes on him. When he flicked a glance back later, he saw the mayor hurrying into the bank.

Fargo grunted and halted as he reached the end of town. He turned the horse and once again peered down the wide main street. Two well-dressed ladies in a buckboard drew away from the general store, and Fargo's eyes moved past the meeting house, the boot repair shop, and the bank. Once again, the thought rose up inside him: something was wrong with the town. He grimaced as again the thought refused to define itself or take on shape and form. But it stayed, prodding at him in its amorphous state. Something was wrong with the damn town, he thought again as he cursed at the stubbornness with which the inner mind refused to cooperate. He turned the Ovaro and rode away at a canter, again realizing that there'd be no forcing the answer.

The day had slid into the afternoon and he decided to scout the mountainsides, noting the few trails a horse and rider could negotiate and the number of sharp ravines and precipitous gulleys that honeycombed the terrain. It was easy to understand how Doc Emerson may have erred and instantly plunged to his death. Perhaps Mayor Frey and the good banker were not entirely lying about that, Fargo mused. But they were nervous about something. The whole town was hostile. It had to fit together somehow, Fargo pondered. He broke off further idle speculation to turn the pinto along the lower foothills until he had rounded the base and saw Apple Valley in front of him.

The sun was dipping over the horizon when he reined up at the Danner place. Sibyl came from the house, her black hair shiny against a pale-yellow blouse pressed tight against her full breasts. Her lower lip was fuller than he'd remembered, but the gray eyes were as sensuously fascinating as when he had first met their penetrating gaze.

"Come inside and say hello to Pa," Sibyl said, and linked her arm in his. "He's just finishing his meal. He always eats early."

She led him into the kitchen of the house, where Mort Danner had his wheelchair against the table, the bottle at his side. His face was already flushed, Fargo saw. The whiskey did little to soften the bitter, harsh lines in his face.

"Good to see you again, Fargo," the man called out, waving the bottle at him. "Have a drink," he said, his speech slurred.

"Fargo will have a drink with me at dinner," Sibyl

77

put in firmly, and Mort Danner's answer was to take a quick pull of whiskey from the bottle.

"Find out anything about Doc Emerson?" Mort asked.

"Not yet," Fargo said.

"Accident," Mort said. "Old geezer should never have been out alone in the mountains."

"Maybe," Fargo agreed amiably.

"Matt's gone to town for the night," Sibyl said, and handed him a dish towel and then a warm, covered clay pot. "We'll be eating in my room. Follow me," she said, and started down a hallway. Her room, at the far end, had the door open. He followed her inside and saw that a small table had been set. He placed the pot in the center.

"You have to see to your pa first?" he asked.

"No. He can get around all by himself. He'll wheel himself into bed soon and finish the rest of the bottle there," she said, no rancor in her tone.

"He drink heavily before the accident?" Fargo asked.

"Not as much," Sibyl said. "But I don't want to talk about Pa. I want to enjoy you." She brought out a bottle of good whiskey and poured a shot glass for him and one for herself. She tossed it down with ease as he watched her. "I like my whiskey hard and straight." Sibyl laughed. "I want to feel the punch of it inside me."

"You like your men the same way?"

"How did you know?" She laughed and opened the clay pot. He smelled the aroma of rabbit steeped in ginger, pepper, and onions. She served him and he tasted the dish, savoring the deliciousness of it.

"Where'd you learn to cook like this?" he asked. "You don't seem the domestic type to me."

"I'm a lot of different types all rolled into one. You go snooping in town again today?" she asked.

"Not snooping so much as letting people know I'm still here," Fargo said. "Something's wrong with that town."

"Wrong? How do you mean that?"

"I wish I knew how I meant it. But there is something wrong with it."

"Because it's such a right proper town tucked up here in these mountains?"

"That was a surprise, but it's not that. There's something else," he answered.

"Because nobody's cooperating with you?"

"No, not that, either. Something else." He frowned. "Something I can't get a handle on yet, but it's there."

"Don't you think you might be imagining a little?" Sibyl questioned, and poured him another drink.

"No. Something's not right."

"Whatever it is, I've never noticed it," she said. "I kept thinking about you last night, about how you handled those two drifters."

"They weren't much to handle," Fargo said as he finished the food on his plate and sipped the whiskey. "Not like you," he added.

"You think I'd be hard to handle?" Sibyl laughed as she pushed from the table and went over to the bed, where she sat down with her legs curled under her.

"You could be," Fargo said. "I think you like to have things your way, on your terms."

"Close enough," she admitted with a smile that was both mischievous and provocative. He rose and sat down on the edge of the bed beside her. She leaned back on one elbow and the lovely curve of one breast swelled up over the neckline of the blouse. "I don't suppose you'll stay around after you're satisfied there's nothing much to find out," Sibyl remarked.

"Not likely."

"Then there's no time to waste, is there?"

"Time should never be wasted. Neither should opportunity," he said.

"I couldn't agree more," Sibyl said, pushing up from her elbow. Suddenly her mouth was on his, all warm electricity, the fullness of her lower lip all softness, pressing, moving, suddenly all moist. He returned her kiss; his hand came against the top of the yellow blouse and felt the warmness of one breast. Sibyl's arm came around his neck, pulling him with her as she fell back on the bed. His hand moved downward, opening the buttons of her blouse. Her breasts fell forward, very full and round and beautifully cupped, each tipped by a brown-pink nipple on a lighter pink circle. His hand curled around one breast, cradling its fullness. Sibyl's lips parted, her mouth drawing him in, and he felt the quick, darting touch of her tongue, moist messages of the senses.

Fargo began to shed clothes and felt her hands pulling at him, helping, pressing against the smoothness of his skin. Her hips moved, legs swinging to one side and her skirt pulled away, her half-slip with it. He took in a slightly curved belly, full hips, a body with a curvaceous layer of fat on it that added to its warm, sensual loveliness; legs not too long but long enough, thighs firm and smooth where they spread downward from the curly, dense V that formed its own triangular halo against her belly.

She turned, let him shed the last of his clothes, and then pressed her warm softness against him. A groan of pleasure rose from deep inside her as their bodies touched. She slid herself upward and brought one full-cupped breast to his mouth. He opened his lips around the already firm brown-pink tip. His tongue caressed, gently first, then harder, and passed over the sensitive top, around the quivering circle. Sibyl made soft groaning sounds, murmurs of desire, and her hands moved along his back with a firm yet soft pressure. He felt her torso move, arch up, and his own warm firmness come against the curly black nap, pressing into the softness of the pubic mound underneath.

"Ah . . . aaaaah, Jesus," Sibyl gasped as she rubbed herself against him and he felt the excruciating sweetness of the sensation.

His mouth still pulling on her breasts, moving from one to the other, he brought his hand downward quickly as her wanting became a flame. She pushed against him in tiny spasms, a little gasped entreaty accompanying each movement. His fingers found her thighs and pressed forward. Her legs fell open and he was touching warm wetness, wonderful, special moistness unlike any other. Sibyl cried out in a short scream of pleasure. "Oh, God, yes . . . yes, Oh, yes, damn," she murmured, and now her hands were pulling at him with frantic urgency. Sibyl was no child of delicacy or patience, he was learning as she pushed hard against him, her flesh crying out in its own way for his touch. He caressed the liquescent walls, more strongly, caught up in the wanting that flowed from her.

"Yes, oh, God, more, deeper . . . oh, Jesus . . . aaaaah," Sibyl cried out, her voice a breathy sound. Her hands pushed against the small of his back. "Take me, Jesus, oh, God, take me, make me, come with me," she breathed in a kind of ecstatic chant as her hips began to rise, fall back and rise again against him.

He felt his own throbbing desire seek, the key finding the portal, sweet wetness, entering, sliding forward. Sibyl's scream hung in the room, a sound of pure ecstasy. She pushed hard against him, in rhythm with his every motion, her thighs wet with the perspiration of passion. She pulled his face down onto her breasts, rolled under him, and gasped out groaning sounds as she pumped with increasing fervor.

"Yes, yes . . . aaah, ah, Jesus, oh, Jesus yes, yes yes," Sibyl cried, the sound deep, coming from some hidden depths.

He felt the dampness of her dense triangle against him, and suddenly the groans grew into gasped sounds. He felt her flesh quiver, her body tighten, thighs opening and slapping back hard against him, her legs twining themselves around his buttocks.

"Now, oh, Jesus now . . . now, oh, God now," Sibyl cried from lips that were open and trembling.

He felt himself swept along with her and let himself spiral inside her. The sweet coming together enveloped him, the senses gratified, beyond discipline, beyond control, beyond anything but the fulfillment of the body. She held him inside her as she trembled and pressed her breasts against his face and found his mouth with one straining nipple. Finally, a shuddered sigh racking her lovely body, she went limp on the bed and only shuddered again when he drew from her. She turned, wrapped her legs over him as he lay beside her, and pressed her lips into his chest. They stayed motionless except for the deep sighs that rubbed her breasts ever so gently against him.

"Reward enough?" she whispered, lifting her head to his shoulder.

"More than enough," he said. "Only it wasn't really a reward."

Sibyl lifted her face and her gray eyes peered at him. "What was it?" she asked.

"Wanting. Hungering. The reward was a good excuse," he said.

The little smile that touched her lips was a shrug of unspoken admission. "I'm glad you're so wise about women," she said. "Now I won't have to bother finding other excuses," she said as she laughed and put her arms around him. Her mouth had just found his when he heard a guttural shout through the closed door and recognized Mort Danner's voice at once. He heard the panic in it. Sibyl drew away, sat up, and reached for a robe across a chair. Her father's voice sounded again, harsher now, words thick and half-slurred.

"He's coming, goddammit, he's coming," the man cried out, and Sibyl was on her feet, hurrying from the room. She left the door hanging open as she ran down the hall. Mort Danner's voice was clear now, slurred words falling over one another. "Got to run. Got to leave," the man said. "He'll be coming."

"It's all right, Pa, it's all right," Fargo heard Sibyl say soothingly. "I'm here. Everything's all right."

"But he knows. He'll be coming. Can't stay here," Mort Danner's slurred voice continued.

"Nobody's going to hurt you, Pa. There, now . . . easy does it," Sybil soothed again. "Easy, easy . . ."

"Can't stay, got to run . . . run," her father moaned, but his voice had grown softer, the panic gone from it.

"No, no, everything's going to be all right. That's it, lay back now . . . go to sleep," Sibyl murmured, and Fargo heard the man's heavy breathing replace his moans and finally he grew still as sleep swept over him.

Fargo was resting on one elbow when Sibyl returned and closed the door behind her. "What was all that?"

"Nightmares. He's subject to them, especially when he's hit the bottle too hard."

"Sounded as though he's had that one before," Fargo commented.

"He has."

"He sounded real afraid."

"Nightmares can be very real," Sibyl said, and he knew the truth in her reply. "But it's over. He'll sleep the rest of the night," she said, and sank onto the bed. She let the robe fall away and sat very straight, her breasts proudly thrusting forward in all their magnificence. "These attacks of his always upset me. Now I'm the one who needs comforting," she said.

"Ask and ye shall receive," Fargo murmured. As his hands closed around her breasts, she fell forward against him. Once again the sweet senses came alive to turn the night into sighs and screams until the little room seemed to throb of itself. Finally she lay still against him, her entire body covered with tiny beads of perspiration. Sibyl slept curled in his arms and he closed his eyes until the night crept into dawn.

He rose quietly, used the basin of water on the dresser to wash, and was dressed when she woke. She sat up, pushed the halo of black hair from her face, and watched as he strapped on his gun belt. He saw an almost mischievous curiosity come into the gray eyes.

"Going to have another go at finding out what's wrong with the town this morning?" she questioned.

"Why not? Somebody in town might decide to loosen their tongue," Fargo said.

"It's a better choice."

"Better than what?"

"Chasing strange shapes through the mountain mists."

"Still can't believe me about that, can you?"

"Sorry," Sibyl said, shrugging, laughter in her gray eyes.

"That's one thing you and Emily Holden have in common," he said.

"The only thing."

"That's probably right," Fargo said.

Sibyl swung from the bed to press herself against him. "Coming back later?" she asked.

"Can't say," he told her. "I'll be back soon as I can."

"I'll be waiting," she said, and stepped back.

He left with a last glance at her full-figured loveliness and hurried into the new dawn daylight. He put the Ovaro into a trot and rode along the base of the mountain. Thoughts of Sibyl rode with him. Emily had said she was nothing but a tease. That sure as hell had been a wrong call. He smiled. The night had been rewarding for more than the obvious reasons. Sibyl knew more about the town than she had let on so far, he was certain. Now that she wanted and waited, now that the closeness of the senses had swept through their relationship, he could draw her out more. Sibyl was still the only contact that offered hope for a lead.

As he reached the end of the base of the mountains, the sun was high and he turned the Ovaro toward town. Parasol was active and busy as he reached it. He rode slowly and drew to a halt outside the bank.

Every time he had met with Myron Beezer, the mayor had been present. Perhaps the banker would be different alone, Fargo thought. It was worth a try. "Anything is worth a try," he added grimly. When he entered the bank, Lucille Todman rose from her desk just outside the open door to the inside office, her thin form unfolding itself hurriedly.

"Just a moment," Lucille said, but he was already striding past her with a nod and into the office, where he saw Myron Beezer and another man. The banker turned as he entered and Fargo's eyes rested on the other man for a moment, taking in a face he didn't recognize yet seemed vaguely familiar.

"Sorry, didn't know you had company," he said, and the banker's round face offered a controlled smile not echoed by his probing eyes.

"That's all right, Fargo. Mr. Smith was just leaving," Myron Beezer said. "In fact, you've met Thad Smith before."

"I have?" Fargo said.

"He was becoming a new depositor the first day you stopped by," Myron Beezer said, and Fargo held the surprise from his face with effort as he glanced at Thad Smith again. The heavy beard was gone, as was the torn hat and riding Levi's. His hair had been cut short and he wore a well-tailored set of clothes. "Thad looks different than when you last saw him. I can understand you not remembering him," the banker said with a touch of pride.

"Transformed, I'd say," Fargo remarked.

"It's our town, Fargo. Folks come here and settle into new ways," Myron Beezer said.

Smith tossed a quick nod to Fargo as he left the office. Fargo waited for the banker to move to the chair at the other side of his desk.

"You've something about Doc Emerson to tell me," Beezer said.

"I was hoping you might have remembered something to tell me," Fargo said. "Just between us."

Myron Beezer's smile was one of chiding amusement. "You mean without Mayor Frey on hand," he said.

Fargo shrugged. "People sometimes remember more when they're alone."

"When they've something to remember," the banker

said, his hard eyes not at all in keeping with his friendly smile.

"Just a thought," Fargo said.

"Not a good one," Myron Beezer finished, and with a nod, Fargo strolled from the office. The short, squat iron safe against one wall caught his eyes again as he left.

Outside, his lips drawn tight, he swung onto the Ovaro. The town's wall of silence was firmly in place, the banker giving firm evidence of that. He rode slowly through Parasol till he reached the other end, where he halted and peered back. His eyes swept the streets, the hurrying figures, the neat houses, and again the feeling pushed at him: something was wrong. He rode on with frustration curled inside him like a bad meal.

Emily was at the door when he reached the house, and he quickly saw the tightness in her face. "I expected you'd be back last night," she said.

"Never said I'd be," Fargo told her.

"No, you didn't. I'll remember not to wait up," Emily said tightly.

"It got late and Sibyl offered to put me up. I thought it best to stay."

"How nice," Emily tossed back. "Of course, the visit was worthwhile, I presume. You learned something to help us get at the truth of what happened to Doc."

"Not yet," he said calmly, ignoring the edge in her tone. "But I will, I'm sure. Sibyl is still the only one being friendly. She'll come around to tell me more. I just haven't tried to press her yet. That could be a mistake."

Emily turned his words in her mind, her lips pursed, and finally emitted a tiny sniff that managed to combine acceptance and reluctance. "Just make sure you don't forget what you're there for," she said.

"Wouldn't think of it." Fargo smiled. "Besides, you said yourself that she's just a tease."

"They're the worst. They can make a man so hot and bothered he forgets everything but the chase," Emily said disdainfully.

"You saying you'd be happier if she weren't just a tease?" Fargo slid at her, and drew a quick glare.

"I'm saying I'd be happier if you'd finish with her and find another lead," Emily snapped, and strode into the house.

Fargo took the saddle from the pinto to let the horse's midsection get some air, and used the body brush from his saddlebag to take off dust and trail scurf as well as groom the horse's mane and tail. He was almost finished when Emily came from the house, the little black bag in one hand.

"I'm going to the Cartsons. Grandma Cartson's feeling poorly. They live some ten miles directly north of Parasol," she said.

"Want company?" he asked.

"I won't need it. It's a straight trail I've ridden before. Will you be back tonight?" she asked.

"Can't say for sure," he replied.

"Another visit to Miss Sibyl?"

"Maybe. Then maybe I'll stay in the mountains by that deep hollow so's I'll be there, come morning," he said.

"Please, not chasing shadows in the mists again. You don't need another distraction."

"You hired me, honey. Don't tell me what I need," he said, and she strode to the barn, her short brown hair tossing as her heels came down hard. Even her neat rear had an angry wiggle to it. She rode from the barn moments later, disdaining to glance at him despite his wave. When she'd gone, he let the pinto rest a while longer. When he saddled up, he rode into the mountains, finally drawing up in the afternoon sun at the four-sided hollow.

No swirling mists now, everything lush and green and the sound of yellow warblers and jays filling the air. He rode to the adjoining slope, where the disappearing victims had been. He found the three deer and moose trails and began to follow them as they wandered down the slope. This time he kept on where he had halted before as all but one of the trails vanished in thick blue spruce. He followed the remaining one and watched it become little more than a vague path, but he stayed with it till he was at the bottom of the hollow. He paused and stared up at the four steep slopes that formed the hollow and then continued to follow the path through a line of red ash until he was suddenly in the clear. He frowned as he recognized his surroundings.

He was at the base of the mountains, on the trail Sibyl had first led him. To the east it led to town, to the west to Apple Valley. Fargo's brow drew into a crease. If the disappearing victims had come down to the bottom of the hollow, they could have gone to Parasol to hide or across the flat, easy-riding land of Apple Valley. But the whole damn thing still made no sense. A rider cloaked in black who shot his victims and then both disappeared. Why, and how? It defied explanation, logic, reason. But it had happened. He hadn't been imagining, tricked by morning mists. It had happened in all its strange, unexplainable reality. Was it somehow connected to Doc Emerson's disappearance? The question remained unanswered. Fargo couldn't even connect it to itself. As dusk began to slip down the mountains, he turned the Ovaro toward Apple Valley.

Night was on the land when he reached the Danner place and Sibyl came out to meet him. "Pa and Matt are just finishing supper. Come in and join them," she said. "Then we can be alone after I do the dishes."

"Sounds fine," he said, and soon found himself across the kitchen table from Matt Danner, the father's garrulousness fed by the whiskey bottle at his elbow. Fargo accepted a bowl of stew and saw that Sibyl's brother still wore the effects of a sleepless night. "Enjoy your night in town?" he asked blandly, and drew a wry smile.

"Damn right," Matt Danner said.

"What do you think about Parasol, Matt?" Fargo asked.

"Good town. A man can get whatever he needs there."

"Fargo thinks there's something wrong with the town, but he can't figure out what," Sibyl cut in, laughter in her voice.

"Wrong?" Her brother frowned.

"Try another word. Different," Fargo said. "Different from other towns."

"How?" Matt asked, and Fargo's lips pulled back in a grimace.

"That's what keeps escaping me," he admitted.

"Seems ordinary enough to me," the younger man said.

"I need another bottle," Mort cut in, and Matt rose.

"No you don't, Pa. You need some sleep," he said, and began to roll the wheelchair from the table.

Fargo's hand reached out and grasped Sibyl's arm as she cleaned the table. "Pa going to have some more nightmares tonight?" he remarked.

"Maybe. Matt will take care of it," she said. "Let's go to my room."

He followed her down the hallway and she closed the door as he stepped into her room. He turned and she was unbuttoning her blouse. "With everyone in the house?" He frowned.

"Not like last night. Quicker, quieter," she said, and the blouse fell from her and her lovely, well-cupped breasts pushed forward. "But it'll be worth it. Trust me," she said, and flung her skirt off.

He shed his clothes and came to her as she fell back onto the bed. Her legs parted, her full thighs wrapped around him at once as she pushed her breasts up against his mouth.

"I kept thinking about last night all day," Sibyl breathed. "Jesus, take me, Fargo, take me." Her almost wild hunger swept over him and he felt himself respond, flesh rising to flesh, touch to touch, taste to taste. She reached one hand out as her screams took on strength. She pulled a small pillow between them and buried her face in it and her screams of ecstasy became muffled sounds.

But her thrusting, pushing, flowing emotions knew no stifling and finally the pillow smothered her long, groaning wail as the moment came, clung, stayed with her quivering thighs until she finally fell back and the pillow slid to one side. "Oh, Jesus, Fargo," Sibyl breathed as he stayed with her.

"You sure were hungering," he said as he finally drew from her and lay half atop her.

"Yes. You're special. I want the most of every minute you're here," Sibyl said.

"I guess I should be moving on before your pa has more nightmares."

"I told you, Matt will take care of him tonight.

Sleep here with me. You can sneak out before dawn. No one will be up then," she said, and her arms tightened around him. She pressed her breasts against his face and curled herself into his arms and slept in minutes. He closed his eyes and slept against the warm, pink-tipped pillows.

He slept hard and she stirred only twice, both times to hold tighter to him. He woke finally as the new day came. He slid from the bed and dressed quickly.

Sibyl woke when he'd finished, and walked to the side door with him.

"I'll stop back tomorrow," he said.

"Not tomorrow. Not the day after, either. Matt and I are taking Pa in the buckboard. He wants to visit an old friend in Puxsney. He can climb into the buckboard and we put the chair in the back. But it'll be a two-day trip there and back," Sibyl explained.

"Two days. You'll be ready to explode by then, if tonight's an indication," Fargo remarked.

"I know it," she said, and let her mouth linger on his. "That's to help you explode."

He patted her very round rear and slipped into the new day. The sun was full in the sky when he reached Parasol. Once again, he slowly ambled through the town, letting everyone who cared know that he was still on the scene. It was becoming a kind of silent game, he realized, one he didn't enjoy. But he'd not come up with any better way to prod things into happening. When he reached the end of town, he halted to look back again. Something was wrong with the proper, ordered town, he told himself again as he rode away in angry frustration. That was getting to be a habit also, he commented with silent bitterness.

He rode the path past Twin Table Rock and finally

reached Doc Emerson's place when the sun was nudging the noon hour.

Emily, in a light-tan shirt and brown riding skirt, stepped from the house, her neat-featured face distinctly cool. "Another night prodding Sibyl? I'm beginning to feel that's the proper word."

"Your thoughts. Your words, honey," he said.

"No matter," Emily said as he swung to the ground. "The job is over."

"What did you say?"

"It's over. You're finished, through. Here's the balance due you," she said, reaching into her skirt for a roll of bills.

"Am I hearing you right?" Fargo asked, unable to keep the incredulousness from his voice.

"You are," Emily said stiffly.

5

Fargo felt himself groping for words as he peered at Emily. "I can't believe what I'm thinking," he said finally.

"Which is?"

"That this is because of the time I've been spending with Sibyl Danner," he said.

"That has nothing to do with it," Emily said, her face remaining coldly composed.

"I'll be goddamned if I believe you," Fargo threw back.

"I don't care what you believe, but it's over," Emily said, and thrust the roll of bills into his hand. "I'm finished, done with it."

"What the hell's got into you?" Fargo barked.

"I've decided not to go on," she said almost loftily.

"Why? If it's not to do with Sibyl, then give me a reason, dammit."

She looked away from his piercing gaze as she answered, took a moment to compose her face into an almost schoolteacher expression. "I've decided what's over is over. Nothing will be changed by my going on. I was wrong to persist this far. I don't like what it's doing to everyone, to the people in town, to myself. I don't want anything else unpleasant to happen. I've decided it's best to end it all right now," she said, finishing with an upward thrust of her chin as she turned her eyes back to him. She had recited the little speech carefully, each short sentence measured out.

"That was a nice little speech. How often did you rehearse it this morning?" Fargo asked.

"I didn't rehearse it at all," Emily snapped with too much defensiveness, and Fargo cursed inwardly. Something was very much wrong, but he knew arguing the point wouldn't bring anything but more denials.

"I'll just pick up a shirt I left inside," he said, and she nodded as he went into the house. She hadn't moved when he returned, but the coldness had gone from her face and in her eyes he saw what almost seemed a plea for understanding.

"I'm sorry," she said. "I didn't mean to be so abrupt. I just didn't want to argue."

"Your show. You call the shots," Fargo said, and her hand came out to touch his arm as he paused.

"Thank you for coming, for trying," she said, and he saw that her eyes held a darkness inside their brown depths. She pulled her hand back as he nodded and walked to the Ovaro. He stuffed the shirt into his saddlebag. He kept his face bland, his voice almost casual. "You know, I've sort of gotten caught up in this thing. I'm thinking of staying around on my own just to get to the bottom of it," he said, and saw her eyes widen with a flare of panic.

"No, no, you can't," Emily blurted out.

"Strictly on my own time." He smiled agreeably.

"No, you can't do that," she said, and quickly caught herself as she saw him raise one eyebrow. "I mean, that would only cancel out everything I want stopped," she said, unable to hide the agitation in her face.

He let himself think for a moment. "I guess it would," he said finally. "I'll just be moving on, then." He caught the quick sigh of relief she couldn't hold back as he climbed into the saddle. "You going to stay on here?" he asked.

"I don't know. I haven't decided that yet," Emily said, and Fargo held the grim smile inside himself.

"Good luck," he said, and put the pinto into a trot. She'd been honest about only one thing: his time with Sibyl hadn't anything to do with her sudden change of heart. But something else did, and he wasn't about to ride away without finding out more.

He sent the horse through a line of hawthorn and oak, turned up a steep slope, and circled back until he found a spot where he could see the house below through the trees. Emily had gone inside. He dismounted and slid down against the thin, brown scaly bark of a hawthorn. He relaxed his body while his eyes stayed riveted on the house. The mountain forests were peaceful, echoing with the chatter of birds, orioles and finches mostly, and the occasional soft brushing sound of deer passing through heavy foliage. The sun had begun to slip over the high peaks when Emily came from the house, Fargo rose to his feet at once.

She hurried to the barn. He was in the saddle when she reappeared astride her horse. She put the animal into a canter as she moved through the woods east of the house. Fargo sent the Ovaro down the steep slope, crossed in front of the house, and picked up her trail with practiced ease. She rode north, he saw, along the side of a gulley that moved downward to where it became a series of small clearings separated by stands of bur oak. She hurried, plainly completely without thought of being followed, and he increased his pace until he could catch glimpses of her ahead of him. He slowed again, stayed back, and saw her go through another line of oak and heard the horse slow. He kept the pinto moving through the trees and slowed only when he glimpsed a house in the clearing that followed the tree line. He moved the pinto to the very edge of the trees and halted to see Emily, her back to him as she stood on the ground and faced three men. Fargo took in the trio with a quick glance: a lanky figure with buck teeth, in the center, the other two nondescript types, one wearing a tan stetson, the other hatless, with short brown hair slicked down with pomade.

Fargo's quick glance saw the blue-gray of dusk moving down from the high land, and he moved the pinto another step closer to the edge of the hawthorn.

"It's done. He's gone," he heard Emily say.

"You pay him off?" the toothy one asked her.

"Yes. It's finished. He's left already," Emily said, and moved so that Fargo could see her face, disdain in it as she peered at the three men.

"He didn't ask anything?" the buck-toothed one questioned.

"He asked, but I had my answers ready," Emily said. "I've kept my part of the agreement. Now you keep yours. Turn over Doc Emerson."

Fargo watched the toothy grin break across the man's face. "We changed the rules, honey," he said. "Now our part is to see that you don't tell anybody what you did."

Emily frowned, the surprise flooding her face quickly turning to apprehension. "What are you saying?" she asked.

"I'm saying you're right, doll. It's over. You're over,"

the man snapped, the toothy grin vanishing from his face.

Emily spun and started to leap onto her horse, but the lanky figure moved with lithe quickness and had his arms around her before she could swing her leg over the saddle. He dragged her from the stirrup and the other two came up to take hold of her as he stepped back. "Bastards! You lied to me," Emily spit at him. "It was all a trick."

Fargo drew the Colt and cursed silently as the buck-toothed one stepped up to Emily, his hands pushing across her modest breasts as he pressed himself against her. The three moved toward the shack with her, all close to her struggling form. Too close, Fargo realized as he holstered the Colt. He swung from the pinto as the three men dragged Emily into the shack.

Night replaced twilight. A kerosene lamp was lit inside the shack as he darted from the trees to the end of the shack, where a cracked, lone window let him peek inside. He saw a single room littered with broken boxes, a pair of torn mattresses, and general clutter.

The two men still held Emily while the lanky, buck-toothed one stepped back and began to remove his riding jacket. "Nothing says we can't enjoy ourselves before we get rid of you, sweetie," he said.

"I'm next," the one with the stetson cut in.

Fargo dropped below the windowsill and, moving on cat-quiet feet, made his way to the open doorway in a crouch. He grimaced. The lanky one was pulling off trousers. The scene in front of him dictated what he didn't want to do. But it seemed he had little choice. He wanted at least one alive and able to answer questions. But if he confronted them, they'd explode with a shoot-out. In the small room, chances were more than good that Emily would take a bullet.

They might even shoot her first. He had no option but to strike hard and fast, and that meant nobody left alive for answers. He swore again under his breath as the lanky one advanced toward Emily. Fargo's eyes narrowed. Maybe there was a chance. The man had shed his gun belt along with most of his clothes.

"Put her on the mattress," the buck-toothed one barked. "I'll take her clothes off."

The two men dragged Emily the few feet to the torn mattress and Fargo saw the fear in her eyes. But she made no pleas for mercy, he noted. As the two others pulled Emily down on the mattress, Fargo half-rose and stepped into the doorway, the Colt in his hand. The toothy one dropped to his knees on the mattress and began to pull Emily's skirt down. Fargo's Colt barked and the one in the stetson holding Emily by the right arm flew back into the wall as the first bullet slammed into him. The one holding Emily's other arm hadn't time to do more than raise his head when the second shot smashed into his chest just below his neck. He fell in a strange, jerky movement as a shower of red spewed into the air.

"Goddamn," the buck-toothed one swore as he whirled and leapt to his feet, his hand instinctively moving to his hip, where he touched only naked flesh. He saw the big man with the lake-blue eyes step into the room, the Colt aimed at his belly. His eyes flicked to his own gun atop his clothes on the floor.

"Don't even think about it," Fargo said, and the man brought his gaze back to the Colt. "On your knees," Fargo rasped, and the man fell onto both knees as Emily rose, pulling her skirt up as she stepped from the torn mattress. "Lover boy, here, is going to give us some answers," Fargo said.

"After this," Emily said, and Fargo saw her draw

her foot up and kick out. She slammed her foot into the man's side with all her strength and sent him sprawling sideways.

"Shit," Fargo swore as he saw the man land almost on top of his clothes on the floor, lash out with one hand, and scoop up his six-gun. He fell onto his back as he brought the gun up to fire from the floor, and Fargo cursed again as he pressed the trigger of the Colt. The bullet tore into the man's naked abdomen just as he began to squeeze off a shot from his own six-gun. The shot went wild and Fargo saw the man bounce up and down on his buttocks for an instant as the slug from the Colt traveled up through his body. He ceased bouncing in moments and lay still, his buck teeth in a final grimace.

Fargo dropped the Colt into its holster as he turned to Emily. "That was a goddamn dumb thing to do," he snapped. "He won't be giving us any answers now."

"I'm sorry," Emily said. "I was just so furious at him. I hate being lied to."

"I know what you mean," Fargo said, and Emily stepped to him, putting her head on his chest.

"I'm sorry, I'm sorry," she said. "But it was different. I lied to you because I thought it was the right thing to do. The only thing, in fact." She clung to him, lifted her face after a moment. "Thank God you didn't listen to me," she said.

He held her for a moment, feeling her warmth and the light touch of her modest breasts against him. A quiver ran through her before she stepped back.

His eyes went to the three lifeless forms. "Let's get out of here. You can spell it out on the way back," he said.

Emily followed him outside and pulled her horse alongside the Ovaro as he retraced steps through the night. "They were at the house when I returned from the Cartsons'," she began. "They said Doc had been taken for good reasons and he was all right. But the people who took him didn't want this blown into something it didn't have to be. That would happen if you kept digging around, they said."

"Simple. Send me on my way, right?" Fargo remarked, and she nodded.

"If I did that, they'd bring Doc back to me," Emily said. "Everything would be back to normal. God, was I a naïve little fool."

"I won't argue with that," Fargo commented.

"All right, but it wasn't just that. It was wanting it to be true. It was relief, hope, a willingness to believe in anything," she said. "Is that so hard to understand?"

"No," he conceded.

"Thank you," she said crossly and then, contrition coming into her voice, "I'm sorry. I did everything wrong, including that last kick."

"You did."

"Dammit, can't you forgive a person, Fargo?" Emily snapped.

"Forgiving is second. Seeing that it doesn't happen again is first," he said as they reached the house. He stabled the horses while Emily went inside and turned on lamps. She had leftover stew and whiskey on the table when he returned.

"It won't happen again, I promise," she said. "I won't do anything or go anywhere without telling you."

"No more house calls, either, for now," he said.

"All right." Emily said, nodding, and after they finished the meal and the glass of whiskey, she came to sit beside him on the small settee. "Do you think Doc might really be alive?" she asked. "Maybe they were telling the truth about that."

He shrugged, unwilling to smother the hope in her voice. "Anything's possible."

She allowed a wry smile. "But you don't think so," she said. "You're being kind to me."

"And you're being too damn smart," he said.

Emily leaned forward and brushed his cheek with a quick kiss. "For being kind. For everything you've done so far," she said.

He turned her face and let his lips find hers. She pulled away after a moment. "No," she murmured. "It would only complicate things."

"Life's made of complications."

"I don't want another till this is over."

"Is that a promise?" he pressed.

"A statement," she returned, and sat back with her legs drawn up under her, the position both neat and somehow protective. But the twin tips of her modest breasts refused to cooperate as they touched the blouse with saucy little points. "What do we do now?" she asked.

"Somebody's tried three times, now and failed. We can't keep waiting for them to succeed. I need a lead, some kind of lead. Think hard, Emily. Didn't the doc ever say anything that would help? A name? A disagreement with someone? Maybe something he had seen?"

"I've been thinking ever since you first asked that. He never mentioned anything to me. He was interested by the town, by everyone in it. He was always fascinated by people," Emily said, and Fargo nodded with memories of his own about Doc Emerson. "Your friend Sibyl hasn't come up with anything, I take it,"

Emily said, and tried unsuccessfully to keep the edge from her voice.

"Not yet." Fargo smiled.

"Then, what next?" Emily persisted.

"More of the same for another day or two. Then I may have to shake something or somebody loose."

"Chasing disappearing riders in the morning mists again?" she snapped out, and was instantly contrite. "I'm sorry. I'm just so on edge."

"I know you still think I was imagining things, but with the leads we have, I can't turn down even my imagination," Fargo said, drawing a quick smile from her. He rose, reached over, and pulled her to her feet. "Time to get some sleep," he said, and as she rose, she stumbled and fell against him, her nicely formed but thin lips only an inch from his. He saw her lips part and felt the moment of her indecision. Then she pulled her lips closed and stepped back.

"Good night," she said, and he smiled as she walked to her room. She had her own quiet self-discipline. But then he'd seen that in the trapper's shack with the three men. She might need all of it before this was over, Fargo thought as he went to the guest room. Strange, deep undercurrents flowed through these mountains and washed across the town. They were there, beyond doubt now. But what were they? The question danced through his mind as he undressed and lay across the bed in the dark room. He went to sleep all too aware that he had only questions and no answers.

The night passed quietly and he woke with the first tiny streaks of gray-pink in the sky. He dressed quickly and hurried to the barn. Dawn was just a promise when he rode from the barn and held the Ovaro at a fast canter through the steep mountain terrain. The dawn mists were still swirling through the deep hollow when he drew to a halt, his gaze scanning the three deer trails on the adjoining slope, searching for a black-clothed rider. But he saw only the wispy gray fabric that was the mist. He silently watched it shred as the sun touched the tops of the mountain peaks. He caught a sound that drifted through the hollow, and his eyes went to the deer trails on the next slope to see a horseman appear, another man close behind him. Both rode slowly, both wearing hats and leather vests.

His eyes flicked to the hollow below. Suddenly another rider appeared, moving quickly, cloaked in black, and Fargo saw the rifle glint in the new sun's rays as the barrel was raised. Two shots reverberated through the hollow and Fargo's eyes went to the next slope to see both riders topple from their horses. He tore his eyes away to peer down into the hollow where the black-cloaked rider was already racing downward into the blue spruce. But he had planned what he'd do. The other times he'd given chase to the rider in black who had managed to vanish into thin air, and when Fargo returned to the victims, they were gone too. This time he'd reverse things. He sent the pinto charging across the steep ground to the adjoining slope. He lost sight of the spot where the two men had fallen for a few minutes as he had to take a narrow trail beside a heavy line of dense shadbush. He pressed the pinto as hard as he dared.

When he drew past the shadbush, he turned sharply on the trail and crossed onto the adjoining slope. A quick glance down into hollow showed that the rider in black had vanished into the blue spruce. Fargo returned his eyes to the place where the three deer trails came close together. When he reached the spot, the two men were still there, facedown on the ground. No disappearing victims this time, he thought as he skidded to a halt and leapt from the Ovaro. He turned the nearest figure on its back and saw a man not much past thirty, lifeless from a bullet that had pierced his chest. He turned the other man over and saw an older face with graying hair. He, too, lay dead, the small stream of red running from the base of his neck.

But the man's vest had fallen open and Fargo felt a frown dig into his brow as he stared at the silver sheriff's badge pinned to the man's shirt. The frown grew deeper and he went into the man's pockets and came out with a square identification card. "Sheriff Roger Thornwood, Cory, Arizona," he read aloud, and turned to the lifeless form of the younger man. He went into his pockets and found another small, square card. "Herman Fowler, Deputy Sheriff, Cory, Arizona," he murmured aloud. He sat back on his haunches and frowned into space. Both men were lawmen. And they hadn't disappeared, as had the black-clad rider's other victims. Why? he muttered under his breath. Why had the other victims disappeared and not these two? What made no damn sense in the first place made even less now. But there was an explanation. He was certain of that, just as he was certain that a horse and rider didn't vanish into thin air.

He rose, walked to the Ovaro, and pulled himself into the saddle. Slowly he made his way back down the steep slope of the hollow, crossed to the adjoining slope, and finally reached the blue spruce, where he had followed the black-cloaked rider before. He pushed his way through the spruce, saw the hoofmarks newly pressed into the earth, and finally came to a halt at the same spot he had halted twice before. Again, the hoofmarks ended, the horse and rider seemingly vanished into nothingness. He scanned the steep stone slabs that rose in front of him. This was part of the mountainside that was fashioned of stone, earth, and heavy brush as it rose skyward. He swung from the horse, knelt down, and ran his fingers over the hoofmarks, which were still damp and absolutely fresh. It was a confirmation he wouldn't ordinarily feel the need to take, but these strange and unfathomable events turned the world into a place of doubt.

He rose to his feet, his eyes sweeping the ground on both sides of the hoofmarks, again just to reassure himself he hadn't missed anything. But, as with the other times, there were no other prints. He turned to stare up at the almost straight slabs of stone that formed part of the mountainside only a squirrel could climb.

"No, dammit," Fargo said, the sound of his voice loud in the hollow. "Nobody just disappears into thin air." He moved forward to where the tall stone slabs rose, overlapping one another, some separated by the steep mountainside of earth and brush, others partly covered by wall moss. He moved to the stone at the far right and ran his hands across its surface, pressing firmly as he did, lifting his arms as high as he could and then bending down to run his fingers along the base of the stone. He moved to the next stone that slightly overlapped the first and did the same thing, firmly pressing his hands across every inch of the stone, from the base where it touched the ground to as high as he could reach. An expanse of earth some three feet wide separated him from the next tall slab, but he did the same thing along the brush as he moved his fingers carefully and thoroughly through the tangled surface. The next stone slab was tallest of all and, he found when he finished, as solid and unyielding as the others had been.

He had moved almost all the way across the straight

wall of stone when he paused before a slab that angled out from the ones on the other side, not unlike a door that touched at both sides but didn't quite fit properly. It was the next-to-the-last slab of stone along the tall slope and he felt the sense of frustration and discouragement stabbing at him. Once again, he began at the right edge of the slab and moved his hands slowly and methodically across every inch of the stone. When he reached the other side, he bent down, ran his hands along the bottom, and then rose and pressed into the stone where it touched the next slab. He stopped, felt his breath catch at him. Something had moved. Or was it just wishful thinking? He pressed again, harder, and felt the movement again, no question of it this time, and the blood suddenly pounded in his temples. He raised his hands another few inches, pressed again, and the slab suddenly swung inward. He jumped back as it continued to swing in until it stopped and he stared at an entranceway some eight feet across and just wide enough for a man or horse to pass through.

"Goddamn," Fargo swore as he heard his own grim laugh of triumph. A rock-lined tunnel appeared beyond the open slab. The black-clad rider and horse had indeed vanished, but not into thin air. They had disappeared into a natural tunnel. Fargo moved through the entranceway, motioned with one hand, and the Ovaro followed him inside. He halted and looked up at the rock ceiling of the tunnel. It was not high enough for a rider to sit his horse but otherwise plenty high enough to negotiate. Fargo led the pinto completely into the tunnel entrance before pressing his hands on the inner edge of the stone slab. Magically, it slowly swung closed with its own perfect, natural balance mechanism, and he was left in stygian blackness.

Stretching his arms out, he felt along the walls of

the tunnel as he began to move slowly forward, the soft sound of the pinto's hooves at his heels. He felt the tunnel lead downward after a few yards, and he kept his hands pressed against the walls. The total blackness plunged him into a strange void where distance became unmeasurable and progress was something he imagined more than knew. But he could feel the floor of the tunnel continue to slope downward as he moved through the inky blackness. The sound of the horse close behind him was the only thing that kept him from wondering if he were not in some timeless void. The walls under his touch remained solid rock, dry and firm, and he suddenly felt the tunnel curve, a slow, long curve, and then again move down, more steeply now.

He moved forward and felt his brow furrow as, in the distance, the blackness suddenly grew touched with faint gray. He increased his pace and the gray took on strength, finally becoming filtered daylight. The walls of the tunnel began to take shape again. The rock roof had remained the same height, he noted as he pressed forward. Now he could see the gray glow that marked the end of the tunnel. He found thick shadbush blocking the way from the tunnel, and he pushed through it with the pinto behind him. He emerged into a glen of white oak and moved through the trees and suddenly he was in the clear. The frown returned to his forehead as he stared ahead where the flat land of Apple Valley stretched out in front of him, Sibyl's house a dark speck in the distance.

He turned and looked back at the base of the mountainside. The rock tunnel had led him all the way down from where he'd entered at the foot of the deep hollow, a direct cut through the mountain. He turned back to stare across Apple Valley. The deer trail he had followed the other day had led him out to the base of the mountains some miles west. But a rider emerging there could well find his way to Apple Valley without trouble. Both trails, the deep paths and the secret rock tunnel, led to Apple Valley, one directly, the other indirectly.

Fargo frowned as an unpleasant thought danced through his mind. He flung it aside angrily, only to have it rush back as if with a will of its own. He swung onto the Ovaro and paused to stare back at the glen of white oak. The tunnel exit was completely obscured. Even someone stumbling onto it by chance would see it only as a cave in the base of the mountain. But the black-cloaked rider had found it, recognized it for what it was—one of nature's secrets—and found a way to make use of it. Fargo turned the pinto and began to slowly ride across the flat land of Apple Valley which stretched in front of him. Angrily, he rejected questions that prodded at him, suspicions that refused to vanish. He felt almost traitorous as he reached the Danner house.

He halted in the front yard. The door opened and he saw Sibyl emerge. Instead of being delighted to see her, he found himself cursing silently, but he swept the anger from his face with an effort.

"What are you doing here?" Sibyl asked as she came toward him, her blouse hanging loose over the top of her Levi's, her full breasts swaying gently under the fabric.

"I was just about to ask you the same," Fargo said as he dismounted. "I was just riding by."

"Change of plans. Matt and Pa decided to go on their own, which was fine with me. I've a lot of chores that need doing around the house," Sibyl said, and linked her arm in his. "But they can all wait, now that you're here and the place is entirely ours."

He walked into the house with her and felt the instant sensuous wanting that came from her as she led him into her room. She turned, took his hands, and cupped them under her breasts. Her warmth seeped through the blouse, her softness both promise and demand. He saw the dark pinpoints that danced in her gray eyes. The questions that had ridden with him still clung, but suddenly they were dim abstractions, swept into the background by the power of the loins. But she felt his moment's hesitation.

"Opportunity should never be wasted. Somebody I know said that once," she murmured, a sly smile touching her lips.

"They were right," Fargo said, and brought his mouth on hers, his hands slipping up under the looseness of her blouse to curl around the full, soft mounds. His thumb rubbed across one pink-brown tip and he felt it instantly begin to grow firm and rise, an echo of his own burgeoning maleness. She fell back onto the bed and he came atop her, pulling off clothes as she wriggled free of the few garments she wore. She was waiting for him when he came naked to her. She reached out for him, stroked, curled her hand around him and caressed. The dark thoughts inside him lay pushed into a corner of his mind by the power of pleasure. Pushed aside but not away, he realized dimly as he heard his own groans of ecstasy when Sibyl came to him with all wet moistness, sinking down upon him to envelop, push, pull, thrust downward again. Her breasts were against his face, seeking his mouth. Her cries, unfettered now, mingled with his own, spiraling into the air, hanging there to mingle with new half-screams. Finally, when the moment exploded, she quivered hard against him and her gasps were sweet sounds of the senses gratified.

"Oh, Jesus . . ." Sibyl groaned finally, and fell to the bed beside him, her breath still coming in deep gasps. He lay beside her and drank in the beauty of her full-cupped breasts and luxuriant body. He let her rest until she finally rose up on one elbow. "I'm glad you decided to ride by," she said, and her lips pressed softly into his muscled abdomen. She drew back, sat up, and swung from the bed. "I'll make coffee," she said, and he watched her walk from the room, her round rear swaying gracefully with every step.

She disappeared down the hall and Fargo swore under his breath as, like so many malicious children, screaming and tumbling and refusing to be kept in line, all the dark thoughts rushed forward inside him. He rose from the bed, pulled on trousers, and stepped to the closet at one side of the room. The sour, traitorous feeling curled itself inside him again as he pulled the door open. Sibyl kept an untidy closet, the floor littered with Levi's, boots, and cartons along with hatboxes and pincushions. Dresses, skirts, and blouses hung from wall pegs and hangers, some lying crumpled on the floor where they had fallen. He stepped into the closet, pushed boxes aside with his foot and leaned down to move scattered clumps of clothing. An oilskin slicker lay in one corner, the bulge of something underneath it. He pulled the slicker aside. A sharp stab struck him in the stomach as he stared down at the full-length cape folded in two, the riding britches, the jacket, and the wide-brimmed hat, everything black as ebony.

Fargo swore silently as his emotions surged through him, all mixed together in an unhappy potpourri—chagrin, bitterness, disappointment, sour satisfaction.

Answers tumbled into place, still not conclusive yet beyond turning away, things unexplainable suddenly finding reason. He heard Sibyl returning down the hall and he picked up the cape and hat and held them behind him as he stepped from the closet. She came into the room, halted, and he saw the frown leap into her gray eyes as she looked at him, instantly catching the expression he couldn't hide. Her lips pursed and he saw sudden caution come into her face.

"What is it?" she asked.

He held his arm out, letting the cape and hat drop to the floor at her feet. She stared down at them for a long moment before lifting her eyes to him. "That rider all in black that you'd never seen, couldn't believe existed," Fargo said. "Morning mists and my imagination come true."

A wry smile touched her full lips. "How?" she asked, needing only the single word.

"I found the tunnel," he said, and she nodded, the wry smile still clinging to her.

"You're real good," she commented almost abstractly.

"I also found the sheriff and his deputy," Fargo said grimly. Sibyl turned, reached out, and drew a robe around herself. "They didn't disappear like the other two," he prodded.

"No, they didn't," Sibyl said.

"Because there weren't any other two victims, not really," Fargo said, and her eyes narrowed as she listened. "The other two men you saw shot were both Matt," Fargo said. Sibyl's gray eyes stayed narrowed but there was no denial in them. "And he was never really shot."

Sibyl's shoulders lifted in a shrug. "We used special cork bullet we made with a very thin tin coating just to give them enough weight."

"And while I was chasing after that rider in black, he just picked himself up and left," Fargo said. "Those other two times were just rehearsals, weren't they? Rehearsals for today."

Sibyl shrugged again. "I didn't know how many Thornwood might bring. I had to be able to shoot and get away. Timing was everything. It had to be checked out."

"Rehearsed," Fargo snapped, and she allowed another shrug of admission. He let a grim laugh well up from inside him. "I actually helped," he said. "I came along and chased after you. I gave your little rehearsals an added note of reality."

"So you did." She smiled and managed to look sheepish.

"I want the rest of it, everything, nothing left out," he growled.

"All right. You've earned it," Sibyl agreed.

6

"We lived in Arizona before Pa had his accident, in Cory. He got into a fight with Jim Thornwood, the sheriff's brother. Everybody knew Jim Thornwood was no good. He came looking for Pa to kill him one night, only Pa got his shots off first and killed Jim. The sheriff swore he'd see Pa hung for it. He wouldn't listen to anybody. We had to take whatever we could and run in the night," Sibyl said.

"You came here."

"In time. The sheriff chased us from place to place. Finally we decided to run far enough so's he'd never find us," Sibyl said. "Only we were wrong. He did find out where we were and set out to come after us."

"How'd you learn that?"

"Matt heard it on one of his trips and then asked around and found out that Thornwood had already set out after Pa," she answered. "But Pa had had his accident. He couldn't defend himself against the sheriff. He couldn't even run now, and Thornwood would make the most of that, we knew."

"So you decided to stop Thornwood on your own."

"That's right, and whoever he had along with him. We heard what direction he was taking and we guessed he'd cut straight through the mountains. We picked a place and began to get ready for him," Sibyl said.

"That nightmare of your Pa's, that's what it was all about," Fargo said, and she nodded.

"He was afraid. He knew Thornwood wouldn't rest. Pa knew he faced being hung or shot," she said. "I decided not to let that happen." She halted and drew a deep breath and he heard the sigh in her voice. "There, that's it, all of it."

Fargo's face stayed hard as he studied her. "How'd you find the tunnel?"

"By accident, plain luck," she said.

"Who else in town knows about it?"

"Nobody, till you," she said. "I wouldn't tell anybody. Liquor loosens too many tongues. Neither what I did nor the tunnel has anything to do with Doc Emerson. Believe me, Fargo, believe me."

"I'd like to," he said, and she came to him, all warm softness.

"It had nothing to do with what went on in this room between us. You have to believe that, Fargo."

"I've got to think some more on it, on all of it," he said, and she rested her head against his chest as she nodded. She lifted her lips, pressed them against his mouth, and finally drew back.

"This is us, nothing else but us, Fargo," Sibyl murmured. He didn't answer but instead pulled back. She watched him dress. "When will I see you again?"

"When I've done my thinking," he told her, and didn't try to hide the grimness in his voice.

She leaned in the doorway as he rode away, her gray eyes still searching his face. He didn't wave. It wasn't a time for waving. It was a time for jumbled thoughts and emotions that swung from anger to uncertainty, hope and cynicism. He wanted to believe

Sibyl. But she had lied to him once. Would she ever have told him the truth had he not discovered it on his own? he wondered. The question hung, casting a veil over everything else she'd said. Still, it could have all been a thing apart, a private matter, as she'd insisted. But did Sybil know more about the town and Doc Emerson than she'd admitted? The riddle of the disappearing black-clad rider had been answered, but nothing else. He still couldn't be sure it somehow didn't touch the riddle of what had happened to Doc Emerson.

The buildings of Parasol came into view and Fargo broke off further futile speculation as he rode into town in the last of the daylight. He rode slowly in what had become a daily visit, a parade of one that he knew was watched both boldly and furtively.

Mayor Frey and Myron Beezer halted a conversation in front of the bank as he paused. "Anything new, Fargo?" Harold Frey asked, an edge of smugness to his voice.

"Getting close," Fargo said, and almost laughed at the shock that swept both men's faces.

"What's that mean, Fargo?" the mayor asked quickly.

"I don't think I'd best go into that now," Fargo said confidently, and moved on. He grinned. Maybe his answer would trigger a mistake. Then again, maybe they'd still hold back. But they wouldn't sleep well, that was certain.

The Trailsman reached the end of town and turned back to let his eyes again sweep up and down the busy main street. He saw Harriet Tilson's ample form walking beside another woman. A well-dressed couple passed her with a nod. Tom Riley lounged beside his boot repair shop, Sam the barber outside his shop. Three women went into the Town Meeting Hall, passing Ben Stoppard as they did. Everything proper, in place, everything that ought to be part of a well-run town with good and respectable citizens. He started to turn away and suddenly pulled his gaze back to the town.

He felt the excitement spiral inside him. The unformed had suddenly exploded into shape, the undefined suddenly given definition. The elusive piece that had never stopped nagging at him burst into place. There were no children in Parasol. Not one damn kid, Fargo muttered. Even rough, untamed frontier towns usually had a few youngsters somewhere around. But not Parasol. Not one damn kid! That's what had bothered him all along, stayed in his subconscious until now. He had told himself again and again that there was something wrong with the town, and that was it.

He turned the Ovaro and rode away as dusk became dark, the excitement with him, the single question tumbling over itself. Why no children in Parasol? Why not a single youngster in a town so proper and respectable? Not a toddler, not a schoolboy, not a youngster approaching his teens. He put the pinto into a trot. Maybe Emily would have an answer, he mused as he rode through the night. It had been a day of surprises, discoveries, and now, new definitions. He suddenly felt tired. Or perhaps disappointed was a better word.

What he had discovered about Sibyl still hung on him like an ill-fitting coat. She had killed two lawmen to save her father from an unjust hanging. Of itself, that was perhaps more to be understood than condemned. But he had only her words for the truth of it, he reminded himself again. She had planned, rehearsed and prepared with cold precision—plainly a young woman of icy purpose. A little more bending of the truth wouldn't bother her. He realized that believing in Sibyl was more than he could muster, and he was sorry for that. His own cynicism, probably, he admitted. Maybe cynicism and disappointment went together.

Fargo finally reached Doc Emerson's house. The lamplight burning in the window made a welcoming sight. He stabled the horse and Emily opened the door for him when he returned, her brown eyes searching his face.

"You look tired," she said. "Something go badly?"

"I'm not sure yet." He had decided not to tell her about Sibyl for the moment. She'd only badger him for his conclusions and he hadn't any to tell her. He hadn't any to tell himself, yet.

"I've some cabbage soup ready," Emily said.

He nodded, sat down, and watched her hurry into the kitchen. She returned with a bowl of soup that smelled as good as it tasted. She sat across from him and waited till he finished. Her quiet directness was strangely comforting. That inner strength, he decided, and he frowned at a sudden sadness he saw in her eyes.

"What's poking at you?" he asked.

"Just seeing you now," she said. "I realized suddenly that this is getting to you."

"In a way," he said. "Different than you think. I don't like not knowing about someone, where they sit, where they measure up, or where they fail."

"The charming Sibyl Danner disappoint you?" she slid at him, and he cursed her female acuteness.

"I'm not sure," he said. "I don't like someone I can't figure. I don't like a town I can't figure."

"Such as Parasol."

"Bull's-eye," Fargo said. "Why aren't there any kids in Parasol?"

"What?" Emily said, frowning.

"Kids, youngsters. There's not a damn one in the

whole town. Never saw any come in or go out, either," Fargo said. "Something's wrong with that town. It kept nagging at me until just a little while ago."

"No children," Emily echoed, the frown staying on her forehead as she stared into space. "You're right! But I never took notice of it till now."

"Doc never mentioned it?"

"No," Emily said.

"He never said there was something strange about the town?"

"Not right out, the way you're saying it," Emily said, and he saw her tugging at thoughts.

"How did he say it, dammit?"

"He used to say that the town fascinated him."

"Fascinated him?"

"Yes. I can remember exactly how he put it one evening: 'Parasol is a town on top of a town,' he said."

"What'd he mean by that?"

"I don't know, but he used a comparison. 'When art experts restore old paintings, they sometimes find that there is a second painting under the one on top. That's what Parasol is like,' he said," Emily answered.

"And he never explained anything more?"

"No, but I remember he seemed amused by the comparison," she recalled.

"He was still learning things, I guess," Fargo said, a grim excitement beginning to spiral through him. "One painting under another. One town under another. Something had to make him come to that conclusion."

"But what?"

"That's the question and the answer all rolled into one. But he had come too close to something, and somebody decided it was best for Doc to disappear." Fargo frowned and put his hands on Emily's shoulders. "Did he keep a diary, notes, personal papers?

The files in his office were nothing, but maybe he kept notes among his personal papers here in the house. Did you look through his things?"

"No," Emily said. "I still hoped he was alive someplace. Going through his things would somehow have been admitting I'd given up. I just couldn't bring myself to do it. I felt sort of ghoulish just thinking about it."

"Well, you're going to do it now with me," Fargo said.

Emily nodded unhappily but took a kerosene lamp and led the way into a neat room with medical books along one wall. She set the lamp on a small desk and Fargo noted a shelf of papers, forms, and folders behind the desk.

"You start on those. I'll go through his desk," Fargo said, and lowered himself into the swivel chair as he opened the first of the drawers.

It held only loose pages cut from medical books on rare and unusual diseases. The next drawer offered only copies of prescriptions dispensed, and he went on to the third drawer to find a collection of pipes, mostly briar and clay but with two fine Meerschaums among the others. He closed the drawer and turned to those on the other side of the desk. The top one held unused prescription pads, the second a collection of empty medicine vials and a stethoscope. He was opening the bottom drawer when Emily put down the last of the folders on the shelf.

"Nothing here," she said, disappointment in her voice as she came to the desk.

Fargo peered into the open drawer to see a thick notebook, large enough to all but fill the confines of the drawer, bound with a leather cover.

He lifted it out, set it on the desk, and opened it to

the first page, where neat, careful script marched across the paper. "Observations and notes since coming to Parasol," he read aloud. Emily was at his side at once, the excitement in her eyes an echo of his own. He turned to the next page and Emily read with him over his shoulder.

June 7
Treated Ed Reiser for stomach pains. Observed long scars across back indicative in shape and depth of those made by barbed wire.

June 11
Visited Harvey Stoller for sprained leg muscle. Observed two old gunshot wounds in left thigh.

July 8
Infection around old scar in stomach of Sam the barber. Scar caused by jagged knife wound. Unmistakable.

Fargo glanced at Emily and she shrugged back as he turned to the next page.

July 21
Called to Tom Riley's place. He had a high fever. Treated condition with agrimony and gun benzoin, recommended alcohol sponging three times a day for a week. Observed old marks on skin around ankles, unquestionably caused by leg irons worn for a period of years.

August 9
Treated Harriet Tilson for her chronic lung condition. This particular condition is brought on by a combination of long periods of exposure to cold and dampness, confinement, and reinfection.
The ailment is often called Folsom's lung because of its occurrence in almost every inmate of Folsom prison.

Sept. 12

Visited Mayor Frey for an acute attack of arthritis. His arthritis is caused by a bullet wound in his neck. From analyzing the scar I'd guess a high-powered rifle made the original wound.

Oct. 6

Called by Dolores Bantry to treat severe cold. During examination observed deep scars along back, unquestionably caused by knife wounds.

Nov. 20

Went to Mort Danner place to relieve spasms and pain at base of spine caused by fall from horse. Treated condition with mandrake and musk. Injury marks not consistent with fall on spine. Instead, observed two gunshot wounds at base of spine. Size indicated six-gun shells.

Fargo paused and lowered the notebook, his eyes growing narrow. Doc Emerson's notes gave the lie to what Sibyl had said. Not everything, but enough to make the shadow longer, belief harder. He was aware of Emily's eyes on him.

"Something she said doesn't hold up?" Emily asked, but there was no tartness in her voice. A gentleness he heard surprised him.

"Doesn't hold up, but doesn't answer anything, either," he said, and returned to the notebook, his eyes moving to the next entry.

Nov. 20

Called by Dolores Bantry to treat severe cold. During examination observed deep scars along back, unquestionably caused by knife wounds. I mentioned scars and she explained them as having been caused by sledding accident when she was a child. Scars were not more than five years old.

Fargo glanced up at Emily as he turned the pages and

listened to her sigh of incredulousness. Each page was more of the same, a meticulous recital of small discoveries. He halted after a few more pages and met Emily's frown.

"What does it all mean?" she asked. "That people have pasts, secrets, skeletons in their closets? We all know that."

"A whole damn town?" Fargo returned.

"I guess that is something more than the usual," Emily said. "Is that what he'd learned, what he was saying in those notes? That Parasol is a strange town full of people with secrets? Is that why he compared it to one painting on top of another?"

"I think he was saying a lot more," Fargo answered.

"And whatever it was, he was killed for it?"

"It looks more and more like it every minute."

"But how can we ever find out what it was? Make whoever did it come after us? That's what you've been aiming for," Emily said. "But nobody's really come into the open."

"And we can't risk waiting longer. We've got to make our own moves now."

"How? Where? What?" Emily demanded and Fargo let thoughts tumble through his mind for a long moment.

"Myron Beezer," he said, and drew a frown from Emily. "He's the only one not mentioned in Doc's notes."

"Doc probably had no cause to treat him, so he never got a chance to examine him," Emily offered.

"That's probably right, but Myron's in a position to know most everything about everyone in town."

'You're saying he didn't want Doc to discover all the things he knows?"

"That's right. If he's controlling the town and everyone in it, he'd want that kept quiet," Fargo said.

"There's a big safe in the main room at the bank. It's used for bank business, deposits, storing monies, gold that miners bring in to change for dollars."

"Nothing unusual about that."

"Nothing at all. But in his inner office he has a small iron safe. Now why would he need two safes?" Fargo questioned.

"One for keeping things specially confidential," Emily said.

"Bull's-eye. I think we ought to have a look inside that safe."

"How can we ever do that?"

"We're going to need three things—tools, time, and luck," he said. "Let's start with the tools. I remember Doc used to relax by fixing things. Did he bring his tools with him?"

"Yes. They're in a toolshed behind the stable," she told him.

"You know what's in there? I need a drill with a bit made for metal."

"There are two or three drills, I know that much," Emily said, and took a lamp from a corner of the room. "Let's go have a look."

Fargo followed her out of the house and around to the back of the stable to a long toolshed. With Emily holding the lamp, he pulled the cover up on the shed and stared down at a jumble of saws, hammers, awls, pliers, and almost every king of tool. The three drills were in one corner, each a different size. He grunted in satisfaction as he saw the largest one had the right bit fitted into it.

Emily let the cover of the shed drop into place and he hurried back to the house with her. She slumped onto the settee and eyed the drill he had put on the floor. "It'll take all night to drill into an iron safe with that," she commented.

"I expect it will," Fargo agreed. "Between midnight and dawn tomorrow night."

"What if we're caught?"

"If I'm caught," Fargo corrected.

"No," she said firmly. "I'm going to be there with you. I sent for you to find out about Doc's disappearance. It's gone in ways I didn't think about. You're in real danger now. I'm not letting you face that alone."

"Done it all my life," he reminded her, and she shrugged away the answer. "Not enough confidence?" he prodded with a grin.

"Too much conscience," Emily answered soberly.

"Conscience can be a burden. Sleep on it."

She rose and came to stand before him, her trim, neat figure a reflection of her inner determination. Directness could be its own kind of beauty. "I'll sleep on it, but I won't be changing my mind," she said, and hurried away.

He went into the guest room, undressed, and stretched out on the bed. It had been a day of discoveries that remained incomplete. Sibyl had been one, Doc Emerson's notes another, and Emily, in her own way, still another. All incomplete, all leaving the final reality still to unfold. He turned on his side and slept with grimness an invisible blanket wrapped around him.

He let himself sleep a few extra hours and the sun was full and bright when he woke, washed, dressed, and smelled the coffee brewing. The day would be a waiting time, the last of the waiting times, he was certain. He found Emily in the kitchen, tan shirt tucked into Levi's that emphasized her small waist. She dished out hotcakes with the fresh coffee. "I thought a good

125

breakfast would be in order, seeing as how it'll be a long night," she said.

"It will be," Fargo agreed. "We take the day slow, relax."

"What if they have the bank guarded?" Emily asked as they breakfasted.

"I'll make it unguarded," Fargo grunted. "But they don't know about Doc's notes. It's not the bank they'll be watching."

"What do you mean?" she frowned and he leaned back and flicked a glance through the half-open door of the house.

"I mean we might have company," he said. "I'll have a look in my own way. Meanwhile, you just go about doing whatever chores you'd normally do."

Emily nodded and his confident smile swept the sudden apprehension from her face. She came to stand before him, and her hands rested on his shoulders. "I'm suddenly afraid," she said. "Suddenly it's not just a suspicion on my part, a determination to find out the truth. I thought that's what it would be, a matter of finding out. But it's not at arm's length now, not just learning a truth. It's danger, killing, murder."

"It never stays at arm's length. You chase a rattler, you can expect it'll come at you," Fargo said.

Emily leaned into his chest, her neat body somehow both frail and strong. "I didn't think it through. I didn't expect I'd be putting your life on the line. I wouldn't have gone on with it if I'd realized that."

"I realized it. I took the job. You're off the hook," he told her.

She brushed his cheek, a fleeting kiss. "Gallantry is appreciated, but it's no match for conscience," she said, then stepped back with a wry smile and began to pick up the breakfast plates.

"Do your chores," he said. "I'll be back." He walked from the house, went to the stable, and saddled the Ovaro.

There was too much forest surrounding the house to find a lone watcher, even two, if they stayed low. But he'd see that they didn't stay low, he muttered to himself as he rode the pinto from the stable. It wouldn't take a lot, just a reversal of the usual, the hare flushing the hounds instead of the other way around. He smiled to himself as he crossed in front of the house, turned slowly, and brought his hand down hard on the pinto's rump. The horse leapt forward and Fargo put him into a full gallop in seconds as he charged east, plunging into a forest of shadbush. He rode bent low in the saddle and kept his head down so he could scan the hills behind without obviously looking back.

A smile inside him came to his lips as he kept the Ovaro at a full gallop. The leaves of the box elder behind him suddenly quivered and he flashed a glance to the left, where a stand of hackberry grew thick. A section of branches moved, a sudden flurry of swaying leaves that became a line of movement as a rider raced through the trees. Fargo laughed, derision in the sound. It had taken even less time than he'd thought. Alarm had galvanized them into action as he galloped into the forest. Since he was racing full out, they thought it had to be something important. Amateurs, he spat, and cast another furtive glance behind him, eyes sweeping the hillsides. But nothing else exploded into sudden movement. Two only, he noted as he slowed the Ovaro, positioned to watch the house from two sides.

He turned up into the hills, letting the Ovaro slow, aware that his pursuers would follow while trying to stay out of sight in the trees. He slowed to a trot as he rode upward, found a small level table of land, circled it, and brought his mount onto the slopes again. They were following, he knew, but they had slowed also, their movements more difficult to pick up. He continued to make a long, wide circle along the slope and finally doubled back to make for the house. He was almost at a walk now, riding casually. He halted at a spot where a big spruce had fallen. He dismounted, drew his double-edged throwing knife from its calf holster, and marked an X into the bark of the fallen tree.

They'd make their way to the tree, halt, see the mark, and wonder what it meant, he chuckled. And they'd fall back another few minutes. Not that it mattered. He was returning to the house, unconcerned with their seeing him do so. But the mark would give them something either to ponder about while they returned to their watching or to pass on to whoever hired them. But he had found out what he'd set out to learn. The house was being watched and there were two watchers.

He had already formed plans for the night when he reached the house and Emily came to the door. He tossed her a broad smile and took the pinto to the stable. She was waiting with her brown eyes wide and full of questions when he returned.

"I was right. We've company," he said. "More confused than they were an hour ago, but they'll be sure to wait around now."

"All night?" Emily asked.

"I'd guess so. I'd make a guess that they'll be joined by others when the night wears on. I'd also make a guess that if we don't go anywhere by dawn, they'll move in shooting," Fargo said. "So that's what we have to do come dark—make them think we're in here."

"How?"

"Got an idea or two. I want to think on them some more."

"Meanwhile, we spend the rest of the day holed up in here?"

"Not exactly holed up. You'll go out and get a bucket of water from the well, set a pot boiling when it gets to be suppertime, everything ordinary and usual," he said.

"That still gives us all afternoon."

"We can relax, nap, laze around. For all they'll know we could be making love," Fargo said, and drew a long, direct stare from Emily.

She turned and went to the two windows and drew the curtains over each, stepped to the door and closed it, slipped the latch on, and turned back to him. "That'll convince them of it," she said, and came toward him. She began to unbutton the top button of her shirt, then the second as her direct eyes stayed on him. "Seems downright foolish to pretend, don't you think?"

"What about those complications?"

"You said we could be killed before this is over. No point in worrying about complications then, is there?"

"No point at all," Fargo said, and reached for her, but she twisted away with a mischievous smile and strode into her room. He rose to follow and she had the shirt off when he entered. She stood facing him, her back to the bed against the wall. His eyes stayed on the slightly shallow breasts first, curved sweetly at the bottoms, each tipped by a very light-pink nipple on a small pink areola. Her breasts were a strange mixture of little-girl innocence and womanly provocativeness. Nicely rounded shoulders and a flat rib cage took his eyes next. Her hands slid her Levi's down and she stood naked before him, a lithe, thin figure, not an extra ounce of flesh on it anywhere, with a flat belly and, beneath it, a surprisingly thick, dense black nap. Beneath the black triangle, legs that, while on the thin side, held a coltish loveliness. In fact, he decided, Emily was thoroughly lovely, with the combination of delicacy and strength of the coral root.

He shed clothes as he moved toward her and saw her tiny gasped intake of breath as her eyes moved across his muscled symmetry. When he gathered her against him, she emitted a quivering cry of delight. He lifted her, swung her onto the bed, and lay half over her, his burgeoning warmth pressed against the dense black triangle. "Oh, oh . . . Fargo . . . oh, oh, migosh," Emily muttered, and her lips came onto his mouth, working with instant hunger, pressing, pulling. He felt the tip of her tongue dart out, hesitant at first, then with sudden, quick eagerness. He brought his mouth down to one smallish breast, drew it in and caressed the pink tip with his tongue. Emily's body rose upward, twisted and fell back again as she gasped in pleasure.

"Yes, yes, oh, God . . . so nice, so nice," she breathed, and offered her other breast. He drew it in and sucked with the gentle soothingness that was so wildly exciting. Emily gasped out small screams of delight. He let his hand slowly slide along her flat abdomen, circle the tiny indentation, and slip down farther until he pressed into the dense black nap.

"Ah . . . aaaaah," Emily breathed as he let his fingers explore and press down onto the soft pubic mound, then down still farther until he touched her slender thighs. "Oh, God, no," Emily groaned even as her legs fell open and he slowly let his hand caress the softness of her inner thighs. "My God, my God," she cried out, and her thighs snapped shut over his hand, forming a soft vise that begged escape. He moved his fingers, letting them stretch between the softness of her flesh, touching the gathering moistness of desire.

Emily screamed as he made contact with the satin-smooth lips. Her thighs fell open and her torso surged upward. She made tiny gasping noises as he stroked, exploring deeper. Her hands were clenched around his neck, pulling his face to hers, and her mouth fell upon his with fervid wanting, touch echoing touch, senses renewing senses until the body was aflame.

"Oh, oh, yes, so good . . . oh, so good," Emily murmured, and her lithe, lean body twisted under his. He moved, came over her, and let himself slide through the dark moistness. She screamed against his face, a cry of sheer pleasure. She arched with him, rose with him, pulled back and thrust forward with him. Her lean body trembled, flesh overwhelmed, unable to absorb the ecstasy of the senses. Her thin thighs stayed clasped hard around him as her trembling grew stronger. Suddenly, Emily's arms stiffened at her sides, her hands became little fists, and a wailing shriek rose from her. "Now . . . noooowww, oh, God, now, now, now," she managed to cry out through her scream. He pushed hard, quickly, letting control be swept away by desire. As she screamed again, he felt her climax encompassing his own.

The world became a void where only the senses dwelled, where only ecstasy ruled, touching, consummating, entwining, only the flesh in control for the sweet explosion that was always too much and not enough.

"Oh, my God," Emily murmured, finding breath, sinking down onto the bed, her thighs still around him. Her shallow breasts still quivered as he put his lips to one and then the other until she finally grew calm. Her short brown hair was damp around the edges and her eyes stared at him with the directness he had come to know was a basic part of her. "I never expected this would happen," she said. "I hope you believe that."

"I do," he said. "But the thought did slide through your mind."

She offered a wry smile. "How do you know that?"

"Am I wrong?"

"No. Something I said? Something I did?"

"Something I felt," he told her, and her smile held a quiet satisfaction. She half-turned, stretched, and he enjoyed the lithe, young-filly beauty of her. He kissed her girlish shallow breasts and caressed the womanly dense black triangle. She fell into a satisfied, quiet sleep and he let himself sleep with her until she woke with the afternoon growing longer.

She sat up on one elbow, her direct stare needing no words. He opened his arms as she came atop him, lean legs drawn up, her flat abdomen instantly rubbing against him. She sought him, fingers curling around him, caressing as he rose to meet her eager wanting. When she sank down on him, she uttered a gasped cry of delight and her mouth found his. He let her set her own pace, held back with her, hurried with her, enjoyed her every gasping, quivering twist and turn, until finally her cry rose into the air, hung there, and finally trailed away in a moan of pleasure.

As she lay against him, her eyes held an unexpected sadness. "I suddenly don't want anything else but you here with me," she said. "And I'm ashamed of that."

"Don't be. You can't stop time. Wanting something different won't do it. Being ashamed won't change

132

anything," he told her, and she clung to him for another moment before swinging from the bed.

"It'll be dark soon," she said, and he reached out and pulled her back to him.

"Another hour or two. Stay here, sleep some," he said, and she returned to curl against him.

"What, then?" she questioned.

"Make-believe time," he said, and she looked at his closed eyes and knew he'd not be telling her anything more. With a sigh, she snuggled in his arms and the house slowly grew dark.

Fargo was first to wake in the blackness of the room. He shook Emily and she sat up. "Get dressed, light at least two lamps, and open the curtains," he said, and slowly pulled on clothes as Emily scurried about. He was almost dressed when she turned the lamps on and light flooded the room. "Act natural. Don't look out the window," he cautioned her as she went to the window to draw the curtain back. "Can you scare up two pillows and an overcoat?" he asked.

"Coming up," Emily said, and while she brought the pillows and coat, he moved a chair against the far wall of the room. He rested one pillow against the back of the chair and plumped the coat up beneath it. He stepped back, his eyes narrowed at the shadow against the adjoining wall.

"I'm going outside. They'll see me get a bucket of water from the well, but I'll really be checking on shadows," Fargo said as he moved to the door, picked up a bucket, and stepped into the night. He walked to the well, filled the bucket, and let himself cross opposite the window. He smiled as the shadow against the inside wall of the room appeared to be the slightly elongated head and shoulders of a person. He returned into the house with the bucket and tossed Emily a broad grin. "Light and shadow," he said. "They can work wonders." He took the second pillow and wedged it into the chair alongside the first and stepped back. Anyone watching from outside would now see the shadowed head and shoulders of two figures. He lay down on the floor and beckoned to Emily and she came beside him. "We crawl around from now on. No shadows besides those on the wall," he said, and she lay still with her hand in his.

"Maybe they've left," she said hopefully.

"Not a chance. Fact is, I'm sure they moved in closer when it got dark," Fargo said. "No matter. They'll think they've got things in hand." He closed his eyes and rested but took care not to drift into sleep. Finally he pulled gently on Emily and she sat up on one elbow. "There's a kitchen window," he said, and she nodded. "Time to go," he said, and crawled to where he had put the drill. He took the tool in one hand and crawled into the darkness of the kitchen, Emily following behind him. He opened the kitchen window an inch at a time until it was just wide enough for him to slip through. Extending his long legs, he pulled himself from the house, landed soundlessly on the ground, and helped Emily crawl out.

He paused, listened, and heard only the sounds of the night—insects and possums, kit foxes chattering in the distance. Moving in a crouch, he led Emily to the stable, helped her saddle her horse, and paused again. "We walk the horses to the back of the stable and into the trees. We keep walking them till we've put a half-mile between us and the house," he said, and she nodded and followed him from the stable. He edged the Ovaro through the open door, alongside the stable in the deepest of the shadows, and kept the horse taking slow, careful steps. He maintained the same, slow pace when he entered the thick hackberry forest. He finally came to a stop and let Emily draw alongside him.

"Ready to play bank robber?" he asked.

"As ready as I'll ever be."

"Hit the saddle, girl," he said, and swung onto the Ovaro.

7

The town was a dark and silent place when they reached it, even the hum of noise from the dance hall beginning to dwindle down. Fargo's eyes searched the darkness as they reached the bank; he halted, listened, and rode closer. He brought the horses to the narrow alleyway at one side of the bank and returned to the front door on foot, Emily close beside him. The bank door was held closed by three locks, and he put the drill to the bottom one first.

"You see anything move, even a shadow, you tell me," he said to Emily, and she nodded and turned her eyes to the street.

Fargo drilled the lowest lock first, then the middle one. They gave way with gratifying quickness and he finally pushed the door open and slid into the bank with Emily. He closed the door after him and put a chair against it. A streak of moonlight afforded enough light to let him discern the teller's window and the partition that separated the outer part of the bank from the inner office. He shuffled along the floor, feeling his way, and finally pushed into the inner office, where he found a small lamp on Myron's Beezer's desk. He lighted it and set it on the floor next to the squat iron safe.

He sat down on the floor, positioned himself as comfortably as he could, and placed the tip of the drill bit alongside the door handle of the safe. He began to drill as Emily sank down beside him, and he was quickly made aware of how long and laborious a task lay ahead as only tiny bits of metal dust fell to the floor. A stiffness came into his wrists and forearms first, then an ache in this shoulders. He shifted positions on the floor but finally had to pause as muscles cried out for relief.

"Let me take over," Emily offered. He handed her the drill as he sat back and stretched his arm and shoulder muscles where they had begun to cramp. He guessed Emily had wielded the drill for perhaps fifteen minutes when she dropped her arms and leaned back. "My God, my wrists are about to fall off and we haven't made a dent in the damn safe," she moaned.

Fargo leaned forward and peered at the spot where they had been drilling. "Wrong," he said, confirming his eyes with one finger against the hole. "We're cutting into it," he said, and she slid back as he took the drill and began the painstakingly slow task. He had to pause again before another hour passed and Emily took over until he'd rubbed the cramps out of his forearms. The procedure became a routine. He drilled till he had to stop and Emily took over until he was ready to continue.

"Teamwork," he said.

"You're being kind," she returned.

But the small pyramid of iron filings on the floor continued to grow higher, Fargo noted even as he could take only a grim encouragement from it. The night was beginning to slide toward the dawn hour, he realized, so he renewed his efforts, though every turn of the drill now brought shooting pain through his arms and shoulders. The hours had been made of painstaking effort and pain, and he found himself cursing the impregnable power of iron when suddenly he fell forward and hit one shoulder against the safe.

"Damn, we're through," he almost shouted, and pulled the drill bit out, letting his arms drop to his sides for a moment and feeling the relief as his muscles relaxed.

"Let me," Emily said as she grasped the handle of the safe door, and he nodded. She pulled it down and he heard the sound of the inner latch give way. The door began to swing open as Emily pulled and he saw the excitement flush her face. The safe door swung fully open and Fargo peered in at two tin boxes inside a surprisingly small compartment. He pulled both out and opened the lid of the first one, where a folded sheet of paper filled the box. He pulled it out and unfolded it as Emily knelt alongside him. A neat list of names and numbers greeted his eyes, running down the length of the first sheet in two columns and continuing onto the next. He had come to know some of the names that appeared on the list, but only a few, and his brow furrowed as he carefully read the columns.

Andy Hillman—$1,000 deposit
Ben Stoppard—$3,000 deposit
Frank Gray—$3,000 in gold (exchanged for dollars with Bank of Tucson)
Harold Frey—$5,000 deposit
Myron Beezer—$10,000 cash deposit
Henry Gruber—$5,000 bearer bonds (exchanged for dollars with Bank of Salt Lake City)
Harvey Stoller—$3,500 in gold (exchanged for dollars with Billings Federal Bank, Montana)

Harriet Tilson—$6,000 cash deposit
Sam the Barber—$1,200 cash deposit
Tom Riley—$4,000 cash deposit
Dolores Bantry—$5,000 cash, and jewels
Abe Henderson—$3,000 cash deposit
Dennis Warren—$2,000 silver (exchanged through Humboldt Savings Bank, Nevada)
Ernie Wright—$3,500 cash deposit
Mort Danner—$7,000 silver and cash
Thad Smith—$3,000 cash deposit
Lucille Todman—$5,550 bonds and cash (bonds cleared through Star National Bank, Silver City)

Fargo lowered the list. There were at least a dozen more names on it. He turned to meet Emily's frown.

"It's a list of depositors. There's nothing to help us in that," Emily said.

"A list of special depositors, including Beezer himself. There are a lot of short-term depositors, miners and trappers, wagon families held here by the weather, passing traders. I watched some go in and out of the bank. None of them is on this list," Fargo said. "But I'll bet they're on the bank's books in the outside safe."

"So why is this list kept in here and apart from the ordinary depositors?" Emily mused aloud.

"And there are no weekly or monthly deposits listed. These are one-time deposits, such as you'd make to establish an account," Fargo said. "And look here, everything that's gold, silver, or bonds has been handled through other banks."

"What's that mean?" Emily queried.

"I don't know. Let's see if anything in this other box will give us the answer," Fargo said, and opened the other tin box, which was deeper and wider than the first. A neat pile of square pieces of paper filled the entire box. He drew them out, thumbed through the top half-dozen, and exchanged a quick glance with Emily.

"They're all Wanted circulars," she said as he quickly ran a glance over the rest of the sheets of paper.

"Every one of them," Fargo said. "Most have pictures on them, a few just descriptions." He watched her stare at the top circular as she read aloud from it, her eyes growing wide with each word.

"Den Dowd—Wanted for the murder of Emmet Story and his family in Utah. Also wanted for three other killings. Five hundred dollars' reward," she read, stopped, and her eyes were wide as they turned to Fargo. "Only that's Ben Stoppard's picture," she breathed.

Fargo read from the next circular. "Wanted—Frank Chowlar, for slaying of two gold miners outside Thompson's Bluff, Utah. Five hundred dollars' reward," he read. "Only it's Harvey Stoller's picture."

"Harvey Stoller, chairman of the town board," Emily commented as Fargo read from the next circular.

"Wanted—Dolly Gant, for prostitution, robbery, and assault. Has run dance halls in Nevada, Arizona, and New Mexico. Used accomplices to rob and assault her customers. Possible murder charges in knife attacks pending. Reward offered in three territories. Contact federal marshals." Fargo halted and pushed the flyer at Emily. "And look whose picture is on the cover," he said.

"Dolores Bantry, from the dance hall," Emily murmured. "You think she's doing that here in Parasol?"

"No, not here."

"Why not?"

"I think we're getting to that, but let's go on some first," Fargo said as the strange pieces began to assemble in his mind. "Look here," he said, and pulled out a flyer with Harold Frey's picture on it. "The good Mayor Frey is wanted in Colorado and Wyoming under his real name of Hal Franey for payroll robberies and bank holdups," he said, and pulled out still another flyer. This one had a picture of Harriet Tilson on it. "Wanted through all the southwest territories," he read. "Maggie Hall, escaped from Folsom Prison two years ago. Wanted for murder of three husbands since escape. Also for stealing their bank accounts. Suspected of other similar murders. Known as Marry-and-murder Maggie."

"My God, Harriet Tilson. Doc was right about her lung condition," Emily said, her voice filled with awe.

"He was right about it all. They came to realize that, in his own way, he had found out their secrets. They had to get rid of him. So he disappeared in an accident," Fargo said, and paused at another flyer. His voice hardened as he read from it. "Reward, one thousand dollars dead or alive for Ezra Kenner, wanted for the killing of Sheriff Hawker in Montana, Sheriff Barady in Arkansas, and Sheriff Hodges in Utah," Fargo muttered, and paused. "Add Sheriff Thornwood of Arizona and his deputy," he said, bitter anger in his voice as he stared at the picture of Mort Danner. But it was Sibyl's face that swam in front of him. She had lied about all of it. Mort Danner was no wronged man, no innocent victim who had fled the pursuit of a vengeful sheriff. He was a cold-blooded killer who plainly specialized in lawmen.

Emily's voice broke into his thoughts. "What do you mean by now Sheriff Thornwood?" she asked.

A bitter laugh escaped his grim lips. "Remember that rider in black I told you I saw?" he asked, and she nodded. "No imagination. No trick of the morning mists. It was Sibyl," he said, and watched Emily's eyes become round saucers of astonishment. He quickly told her what he had discovered, skipped over the details of how and when, and recounted how Sibyl had explained what she had done. "I guess I wanted to believe that part of it," he said. "Nobody likes to think they've been taken entirely."

"I'm having trouble believing any of this," Emily said, and he brought his gaze back to the remainder of the flyers.

"Information is that Kenner was badly wounded during the last gunfight with Sheriff Hodges and may be crippled or walk with a bad limp. He is accompanied by a son, Matt, and a daughter, Sibyl Kenner," Fargo finished. Anger curling inside him, he rifled through the rest of the circulars and suddenly halted, pulled one out of the others. The picture of Myron Beezer stared back at him. "Here it is, the icing on the cake," Fargo said. "Wanted—Max Barry, for embezzlement of twelve thousand dollars from the Bank of Omaha, Nebraska, and possible killing of a bank clerk." He paused, pulled out the flyer beneath it. "One more," he snapped bitterly. "Wanted for robbery and embezzlement, Lucille Todman, believed accomplice of Max Berry."

Fargo dropped the flyers into the tin box and met Emily's shocked stare. "They're all here, Abe Henderson, Sam the barber, Tom Riley, all the good and solid citizens of Parasol," he said.

"That's what Doc meant by his comparison, one painting underneath another. Parasol is made up of people who aren't what they seem to be," Emily murmured, shock still curled in her voice.

"It's more than that. He said Parasol is a town on top of a town, and that's exactly what it is. The whole town was established to give these killers, bank robbers, holdup men, and assorted criminals a place not only to hide but to find a way to use what they'd stolen. Most of them couldn't deposit their stolen money, gold, or silver in an honest bank and draw on it without risking questions and discovery. Running from the law with their loot was also risky and pointless. In Parasol, they could change their identities, become respectable citizens, and deposit their money in a bank where no questions were asked. More important, as an established bank, even one stuck up here in these mountains, it could make connections with other banks and clear gold, silver, and bonds legitimately. I'd guess the whole town was Myron Beezer's idea. He needed a haven for himself, but he couldn't do it alone. He sent word out along the underground grapevine and the town was born—a very proper, respectable town indeed."

Fargo leaned back and Emily ran a hand through her hair as she let the enormity of his words sink through. "Now that we know, what can we do?" she asked.

"I know a half-dozen federal marshals who'll be real happy to know about the good citizens of Parasol. We take what we have here and run like hell with it," Fargo said.

"Can we get back to the house so I can pick up some things?" Emily asked.

"We'll find a way," Fargo said when a sound rumbled through the predawn darkness—hoofbeats, galloping horses, at least a dozen. "Shit," he swore as he blew out the lamp.

"It's them, isn't it?" she said. "How did they know?"

"They didn't. They took a guess. The ones watching the house finally got suspicious. I was afraid they might when the shadows didn't move all night," Fargo said. "They crawled close enough to look in. But then they had to report first. That's why they took till now to get here." He rose and pulled her with him as he dashed through the darkness inside the bank. The sound of the hoofbeats grew closer as they reached the door. He raced outside and into the blackness of the alleyway where the horses waited.

Emily kept pace with him as he sent the Ovaro out the rear of the alleyway and crossed the short open space into a stand of white oak, where he reined to a halt and listened. Muffled shouts drifted through the darkness and he cast a glance at Emily. "They're inside the bank. Now they know that we know," he said, and put the Ovaro into a trot.

"Where? They'll be out looking for us, won't they?" Emily asked.

"You can be damn sure of that," he snorted. "They're retired killers, but they're still killers. We'll go back to the house for now."

"To the house?" Emily echoed, protest in her voice.

"It's the one place they won't expect we'll go," Fargo said. "We'll pick up your things and figure out what to do, come dawn."

"That won't be far off," Emily said, and he nodded as he saw a faint touch of gray over the distant mountain peaks. He set a fast pace and it was still dark when they reached the house. He leaned against one wall as Emily threw clothes into her travel bag. "I think I'm being an optimist," she muttered as she put away the last blouse, "I may never get to wear these."

"You might not," he said honestly, and she made a grim face. But his thoughts were tumbling over one another as they had during the ride back from the bank. Their past would return to them quickly enough. They knew about pursuing and being pursued, all of them. They'd spread a dragnet over the entire area with agreed-upon signals for whoever spotted him. At a signal they'd close the net from all sides. They couldn't afford to let him get away. They'd give chase and go full out as soon as he was spotted. They'd want him first, certain they could pick up Emily any time afterward.

He'd have only one chance, he reckoned. He had to use the anxious pursuit against them, turn it back on them. The fox had to turn the chase against the hounds.

He saw the gray of dawn begin to slide across the sky, and he turned to Emily. "What have you got around here that'll catch fire quickly?" he asked, and she sent him a questioning glance. "I haven't time for explanations now. Just answer me."

"I've two sacks of cooking grease. That'll burn quick, but it'll smoke and smell something awful," she said.

"That won't bother me any. Anything else?"

"Doc has a dozen bottles of rubbing alcohol. That'll catch quickly. There's some benzene and a sack of axle grease in the barn," she said.

"Pour all the alcohol into one sack. Pour the benzene over the axle grease," he said. "I saw some thick paintbrushes in the toolshed. I'll get them. Move, honey. Every second counts now." He hurried behind the stable to the toolshed, found two wide paintbrushes, and pushed them into his belt. When he returned to the house, Emily handed him a heavy burlap sack that dripped from the bottom.

"The alcohol," she said, and hurried past him to return a few minutes later with another heavy sack. "Axle grease and benzene. I'll get my cooking grease," she said, hurried into the kitchen, and returned carrying one more heavy sack. He tied two of the sacks around the saddle horn of her horse and let her carry the third across her legs as she rode from the house beside him. "I become a pack mule all of a sudden?" she asked with an edge.

"If they spot us, I want to be able to race away and take them with me," he said. "And you're the one who'll be using those sacks."

She fell silent and rode beside him as he sent the pinto into the mountains and across the trails to where he finally reached the deep hollow. The morning mists still swirled as the new sun began to break over the high peaks. He led Emily halfway down the first slope and halted, his gaze reaching out to the adjoining slope where the sheriff and his deputy had been slain.

"These trees are dry enough to burn quickly, but we can't take chances. I want a fire blazing hot in minutes," he said. "You're going to make a circle across all four of these slopes and you're going to brush everything you have in those sacks on each slope. I'd guess you have enough to go around if you brush every sixth tree or bush, and that's all it'll take."

"To do what?"

"To set all four of these slopes into a roaring forest fire in seconds. The wind whips down into the hollow. It'll send the flames racing down the slopes like a stampede of buffalo," he said, and handed her the two paintbrushes. "Use these. Don't try to be neat. Just brush over the leaves and branches as best you can and keep going. It won't matter if you run out before you've completely covered the last slope. You'll have spread on enough."

"Then what do I do?" she asked.

"You come back here and stay in the trees," he said, and gave her a box of matches from his saddle-bag. "Take these," he said. "When the time comes, toss them lighted onto as many of the nearest trees and shrubs you've brushed."

"When the time comes? How will I know that?"

"When you see them chasing me down this slope," Fargo said. "You wait till they've all passed the circle you've brushed before you get this whole damn hollow ablaze."

"What are you going to do now?" Emily asked.

"Play pied piper." He tossed her a grin.

He started to turn the pinto when she called out, fear in her voice. "You can't do this," she said.

"Do what?"

"You lead them down into this hollow and you'll be trapped at the bottom with the rest of them," she said. "I can't let you do that just to save me."

He hesitated, saw the real caring in her brown eyes. She thought he was doing the noblest of all things. He couldn't disillusion her. It wouldn't be right, he told himself. But one didn't turn down the mantle of nobility. Besides, there was more than enough danger. Something could always go wrong. "I think I can come out of it. They'll try to escape and fight their way out and pay the price. I'll hang back," he said, and she leaned forward, her lips finding his.

"Come back, Fargo. Please come back," she sobbed.

"Go to the house after you set things blazing," he said. "I'll find a way back."

She nodded and he rode away, pushing aside a stab

of guilt. He halted halfway up the slope to watch her moving along with the paintbrush, then he turned and rode on again. He was indeed going to play pied piper, but not yet. He estimated it'd take over an hour for Emily to circle the four slopes and he'd stay hidden till then. He rode cautiously through the new morning and found a heavy thicket of red ash, where he dismounted and settled down to wait. Harold Frey and Myron Beezer would be taking a direct part in the chase, he was certain, and a wry smile edged his lips. He'd been chased by plenty of cutthroats but never by a whole town. Mort Danner was probably the only one who wouldn't be taking part in the search. Maybe Sibyl would stay back with him, Fargo reflected. He grimaced as she stayed in his thoughts.

She had told him the truth about only one thing: she'd killed to protect her father. All the rest was a lie, and that made her little better than Mort Danner. He spat and wiped the sourness from his mouth. He'd wrestle with what to do about Sibyl when it was over. If he were around to wrestle with anything, he reminded himself as he closed his eyes, letting his body relax. He sat up again only when the sun had moved almost directly overhead. He rose and climbed onto the pinto, pushed out of the thicket, and moved up into higher land. He rode boldly into the open along a ledge and reined to a halt as a horse and rider appeared. The rider saw him and instantly drew his six-gun, though he was far out of range.

Fargo smiled as he watched the rider shoot two quick shots into the air. The signal had been given, the quarry sighted, and the rider started to move toward him. The Trailsman started to wheel the Ovaro in a circle when he was surprised to see two more riders appear from below the ledge, a dozen yards closer. He recognized one as the boot repair man, Tom Riley, and he put the pinto into a quick gallop along the ledge.

The three riders swung in behind him to give chase. He led the way onto higher ground, took a steep incline, and reached the top just in time to see four more horsemen charging toward him. He recognized Ben Stoppard and Sam the barber in the lead, and he swerved again and plunged down to a narrow mountain gulley. A volley of shots sprayed wildly behind him.

Fargo reached the end of the gulley to see a band of six more pursuers racing at him from the north. They had done a better job of saturating the mountains than he'd expected, and he sent the pinto off in another direction. He plunged into a heavy stand of hackberry and halted. He pulled the big Sharps from its saddle case, raised it to his shoulder, and waited. There was no reason not to cut the odds a little and slow them down for a moment.

The six pursuers entered the thick hackberry and slowed. Fargo drew a bead on a wide-set rider on the left, a shadowy shape amid the foliage. He fired a single shot and the rider toppled sideways from the horse. Fargo saw curly brown hair tumble down as the figure's hat flew off, the broad face clearly visible for an instant. "Harriet Tilson," he muttered. "Shit, I was right. It is the whole damn town." He swung the rifle, fired two more shots, and another figure fell from his horse as the others reined up and turned to take cover. He pushed the rifle back into its saddle case and sent the Ovaro streaking through the trees to emerge onto an open stretch of high land. He flung a glance behind him to see the riders come out of the hackberry as another band of at least eight appeared from the north and charged down the open terrain.

He recognized Harold Frey in the lead and, to his left, Myron Beezer. Another quick glance let him pick out Harvey Stoller and Abe Henderson. A fourth set of riders came into view from south on a ridge, some probably hired guns, Fargo guessed. It was time to lead the hounds to the hollow, he decided. They had done too good a job of positioning themselves in the mountains, and he bent low in the saddle as a volley of bullets flew over his head. He changed direction again and cut through a line of hawthorn, following a deer path across a wooded stretch until the mountain hollow came into sight, its four slopes surrounding it on all sides. He glanced back and flung a triumphant oath into the wind as he sent the Ovaro down the nearest slope.

They'd have to slow as they followed, he knew. None of their horses could match the pinto's balance and sure footedness. But they were pressing their mounts recklessly, he saw. Or perhaps it was a mixture of eagerness and desperation. They dared not let him get away and they were certain he was about to box himself in. He sent the pinto down the steep slope and passed the halfway mark, then slowed and managed to catch a glimpse of the black patches of grease on the tree branches. Four of his pursuers had outdistanced the others and were crowding him. He drew the big Colt and fired as he kept the pinto moving downhill and saw one of the riders seem to catapult from the saddle. Another tried to swerve and his horse lost its footing and went down, and Fargo saw the rider half-dive, half-fall from the saddle. The other two slowed and the Trailsman returned his concentration on negotiating the steep slope. He felt the pinto's front feet slip and he leaned back in the saddle to help the horse regain its balance.

Most of the others had split into two groups, he saw, one charging down the slope after him headed by Myron Beezer, the other moving down the adjoining slope led by Harold Frey. Fargo cast a glance past his pursuers, halfway up the mountainside, and the oath fell from his lips as the foliage remained quietly peaceful. "Now, dammit," he hissed, ducking low as a half-dozen shots sprayed the air near him. His quick glance at the two groups of pursuing riders told him that most of Parasol made up those racing after him. He glanced downward to where the bottom of the hollow was growing closer by the second. The sudden hissing sound came to his ears and he turned in the saddle to see the slope behind him erupting in a blazing wall of fire. The flames, pushed by the wind, spread to the next slope and then the other two until the hollow was ringed by a necklace of leaping flame.

He saw his pursuers rein to a halt to stare upward to where all four slopes were now burning furiously, the wind sending the flames racing downhill, catching on dry brush to leap up with renewed fury. He felt the heat as the hollow quickly became a fiery mass of flame, a circular wall that cut off all escape. "I'm getting out of here," he heard one of his pursuers shout, and another took up the cry. He looked back and saw that more than half the men chasing directly after him had turned their horses and were charging back toward the flames. At least as many on the adjoining slope had also turned back. As he watched, they tried to find a place to break through the ring of leaping flames. But there was no place; their horses shied away, spilling some to the ground as others cringed back from the searing heat. One rider, Abe Henderson, forced his horse forward to try to race through the flames, and his screams of pain echoed through the hollow as his horse raced back alone and in panic.

Fargo glanced across at the adjoining slope to see that Harold Frey had outraced his men and, reaching the bottom of the hollow, had turned his horse and was charging toward him. The line of thick blue spruce lay directly ahead and Fargo moved toward it, then slowed and unholstered the Colt and fired a shot at Frey. But the man lay low over his horse's withers and the shot missed. Fargo turned away from the spruce as he reached the bottom of the hollow and charged to meet Harold Frey. He holstered the Colt and yanked the big Sharps from its saddle case, but he didn't try firing as Harold Frey swerved his horse from side to side, coming at him with almost undiminished speed. The others would reach the bottom of the slopes soon, the flames racing at their heels. Seconds were becoming increasingly important. He didn't have time to squander on Harold Frey, and when he saw the man's hand come up with the six-gun in it, he kept the Ovaro charging directly at the other horse.

He saw the moment of uncertainty come into Harold Frey's eyes and the man pulled on his reins, turning his horse enough to avoid a head-on collision. But he kept his gun raised and Fargo swung half around the other side of the Ovaro's neck and the bullet whistled over his head. He swung back, yanked hard on the reins, and the pinto wheeled in a tight circle. He was charging Harold Frey as the man was still bringing his horse around. Holding the stock of the rifle in front of him, he smashed it into Harold Frey's face as though it were a blunt lance. The mayor's face erupted in a shower of red as he fell from his horse. He was lying on the ground, dazed and bloodied, as Fargo raced on toward the blue spruce again.

The bottom of the hollow was quickly turning into a caldron of heat and flame, but he knew the others would race into the spruce after him, hoping they'd kill him and the fire would somehow burn itself out. Fargo, head lowered, raced the pinto through the spruce. He had perhaps a minute before they'd catch sight of him again, he estimated. He leapt from the horse before it came to a halt as the wall of rock and earth rose up before him. He ran to the far end of the rock, pressed his hands along the bottom edge, and the slab of stone swung outward on its natural fulcrum. He swore as it swung with agonizing slowness, and it was just barely open enough for him to squeeze through with the Ovaro when he led the horse into the tunnel. He pressed the inner edge of the stone and it began to swing closed again.

The stone slid back into place and he waited for a moment in the pitch blackness. He could hear the shouts from outside, dim sounds that told him they had reached the wall of stone and earth and were racing back and forth in confusion just as he had done often enough. But the shouts changed character, becoming screams of panic. The roaring flames were sweeping the bottom of the hollow now, he knew, cutting off all escape. Myron Beezer and the others would try to race through the flames. They had no choice left, but the results would be the same as if they stayed—suffocation and fiery death. Fargo turned and began to make his way down the inky blackness of the tunnel, the pinto following on his heels.

The passage seemed longer than he remembered it

being. Perhaps because he was not driven forward with excitement and discovery this time, he reflected, only an overwhelming feeling of relief. But the first grayness of light finally appeared and he hurried forward to where the tunnel neared its end and the light filtered through enough to give shape to the rock-lined walls and roof. The dense covering of shadbush that hid the exit of the tunnel came into view and he pushed his way through it. He had just reached the stand of white oak that followed the thick shadbush when he heard the voice call to him, anger wrapped in ice, and he halted.

"That's far enough, Fargo," it said, and he saw Sibyl step from behind a tree, a rifle in her hands. "Drop your gun," she ordered. "Very carefully." He obeyed, lifting the Colt from its holster with two fingers and letting it fall to the ground. Sibyl's sensuous face was drawn tight, her eyes gray ice. "Walk ahead of me," she said, and gestured with the rifle, falling in a half-dozen steps behind him. "Don't get smart. I'm an excellent shot. But I'm sure you remember that."

"I remember," Fargo said.

"You bastard. Matt was one of the riders chasing you."

"His mistake," Fargo tossed back coldly. It was past time to try to placate her, he realized.

"Son of a bitch," Sibyl hissed. "It was too late for me to stop them when I'd realized what you'd done," she said, and he heard the bitter fury in her voice. "I was watching from the high ridge. I knew you were trying to reach the tunnel, but I was sure they'd catch up to you before you got to it."

"And suddenly you saw the fire explode around the whole damn hollow," Fargo said, not trying to hide the victory in his tone.

"That's right, you bastard. I couldn't get to them any longer. The damn flames were jumping sky-high in seconds," Sibyl said. "Then I saw Myron and the others slow to look back at the flames. I knew then they'd given you the few extra minutes of time you needed to reach the tunnel ahead of them."

"So you raced down and around the base of the hills to get here," he said. "A reception committee of one."

"Exactly," she snapped.

"What are you waiting for? Why don't you pull that damn trigger?"

"I'm going to let Pa do that," Sibyl said, and he turned to glance back at her.

"Never shot a man you screwed? An attack of sentiment?" he asked as his eyes gauged the distance between them.

"Shut up, damn you," Sibyl said. "And keep walking."

He turned and moved on. The rifle in her hands hadn't wavered, the distance between them a foot too long. He kept walking until suddenly he was out of the trees and into clear land. Another stab of surprise shot through him as he saw Mort Danner in his wheelchair atop a small incline, the buckboard in the distance. He cast a questioning glance at Sibyl.

"Pa wanted to come along and get together with everybody when it was over," she explained. "I told him to wait here. The buckboard wasn't going to make it into the high land."

Fargo turned back to where Mort Danner frowned from his wheelchair. "What the hell's all this?" the man growled at his daughter.

"Matt's dead. They're all dead," Sibyl said. "He outsmarted them."

"Matt dead," Mort Danner echoed hoarsely, his eyes burning into the big man in front of him. "You goddamn bastard. This is the end of the road for you." Mort Danner turned the wheelchair around. "Bring him over here, girl," he barked at Sybil. "And give me that rifle."

"You heard him. Move," Sibyl ordered, and Fargo stepped toward the wheelchair, his eyes narrowed. The chair was at the very top of the incline, he saw as he began to cross in front of it. His thoughts raced. Life or death depended on a desperate guess on the power of human relations and the instantaneousness of automatic reactions. The Danners were a tight-knit clan. Love was very real, albeit in its own, twisted amoral fashion.

He reached the front of the wheelchair as he moved past, gathered himself for a split second, and then exploded in a burst of muscled energy. He kicked out with his left leg as he dived forward, his foot slamming hard into the wheelchair. He heard Mort Danner's shouted curse of surprise mingle with Sibyl's scream. He looked back as he hit the ground and saw the wheelchair flying back down the incline and Sibyl leaping after it. He was on his feet as she reached it, her hands wrapped around the armrest and her feet digging into the ground to bring the chair to a halt.

Fargo charged at her and she saw him coming just as she brought the chair to a stop. She tried to turn to meet his charge and bring up the rifle, but he was bowling into her in a headfirst tackle. She went down with him and he heard Mort Danner scream as the wheelchair gathered speed again and careened down the incline. Sibyl clawed at Fargo and he ducked away as she twisted, rolled, and paused for an instant to look on in horror as the wheelchair slammed into a boulder at the end of the incline. Fargo saw it shatter into pieces and Mort Danner's heavy body fly upward and smash sideways against the rock. Sibyl's scream of anguish was cut short as she rolled, dived, and Fargo saw her hands close around the rifle.

He flung himself sideways as she fired from an almost prone position, the shot going wild. He rolled, saw her come up on one knee and fire again, but he managed to dive left and felt the shot graze his shoulder. He hit the ground, came up in seconds, aware that the rifle didn't hold another shot. Sibyl, the gun in one hand, ran for her horse. She flung herself onto the saddle and raced back through the trees as he ran for the Ovaro. She was into the white oak before he reached the pinto and turned to go after her. He heard her crashing through the shadbush ahead, racing for the tunnel. He saw her horse outside the exit when he reached it—she'd raced inside on foot to make better time. He swung to the ground and plunged into the tunnel after her. He'd no time to search for where he'd dropped the Colt, he swore under his breath as the tunnel quickly assumed its stygian blackness.

He paused, listened, tried to hear her ahead of him, but there was only silence. She could be moving on soundless steps, hoping to reach the other end of the tunnel and lose herself in the smoke and smoldering remains of the hollow until she could find her way higher into the mountains. Or she could be waiting for him in the pitch blackness of the tunnel. He swore under his breath as he moved forward carefully, holding his arms out in front of him. The total blackness seemed an invisible wall with no way of knowing what lay behind or before it. He inched forward and felt tiny beads of perspiration form on his forehead. She still had the rifle, empty or not, he reminded himself. The long curve of the tunnel began to straighten and he ran one hand along the rock wall to follow the invisible path.

He paused again to listen, heard nothing, and started forward. He'd gone perhaps another few yards when his outstretched arms touched something and he moved his hand and felt the smoothness of thick hair. The rifle stock smashed into his groin as the narrow tunnel suddenly exploded in fury. He fell back in pain, went down on one knee, and felt himself bowled over backward as Sibyl smashed into him. The rifle came down again with blind, wild swings, but the narrow tunnel made it impossible for her not to hit somewhere on him. She was screaming and cursing now, a wild tigress clawing, hitting, and kicking in the blackness.

He let himself roll backward, but she was on him and he felt her knee come down into his side. He got one arm up, wrapped it around her leg, and pulled, and he heard her gasp of pain. "Bastard. I'll kill you," she cursed. He felt her teeth sink into his arm and it was his turn to curse in pain. He pulled his arm back, covered up, and felt her rain kicks and blows on his back. His heels braced against the floor of the tunnel, he exploded forward and smashed swinging, looping blows into the blackness. He felt his fist hit skin and bone. Sibyl gasped in pain and he heard her fall. He groped, reached down, and felt her knee come up and slam into his thigh. He drove another blow downward and his fist sank deep into her midsection. She groaned and her legs rolled against his ankles. He reached out, felt her arm come up, and smashed another pile-driving blow downward. This time he felt his fist crash into her jaw and heard the snap of her jawbone as she went limp.

He reached down, found her sleeve, and moved his hand down to close around her forearm. He rose and began to drag her with him down the tunnel. He halted only when the light filtered grayly into the passage as he reached the opening. He looked down at Sibyl. She was still unconscious, her jaw hanging limply to one side, and he dragged her from the tunnel and into the shadbush. She stirred when he reached the white oak and he let her drop to the ground while he began to search for the Colt. He was poking through the grass with one foot when he heard movement behind him. He turned, to see Sibyl, her jaw swollen and hanging loosely, her eyes burning with a wild glow, charging toward him. He tensed, waited, and suddenly saw the knife in her hand. He managed to fling himself sideways as she lunged forward with the blade. He flung out one leg with his back half-turned from her.

She stumbled, fell forward, hit the ground, and he heard the long, groaning gasp come from her. She stayed with her face pressed into the earth and he stepped toward her, carefully leaned down as he expected her to whirl and spring at him again. But she lay still, and he closed one hand on her shoulder, pulled, and turned her onto her back. He grimaced as he saw the hilt of the knife protruding from between her breasts and her gray eyes staring lifelessly upward. He drew a deep breath and turned away, the sourness curling inside him again. Up to the very last, he'd subconsciously hoped there'd be a different ending for Sibyl Danner. But it had been a hollow hope. Blood, loyalty, family, they were all invisible chains only a very few could break.

He walked back to where he'd been searching for the Colt, finally found it, and pushed the gun into its holster. He returned to the Ovaro, paused, and decided not to go back through the tunnel. It was by far the shorter way back to Doc Emerson's house, but he'd had enough of the finality of death. Instead, he rode slowly around the base of the mountains, passed the town, and paused to scan its almost deserted streets with only a few pack mules tied to a hitching post. He made his way on, passed Twin Table Rock, and finally climbed to the neat house in the clearing as the sun slid into the afternoon.

He had reached the door and dismounted when Emily came out, her eyes wide, and suddenly she was in his arms, clinging to him. "You're back! Oh, God, you're back," she said. "I never thought I'd see you again." Her mouth pressed his, a long, trembling kiss. "I watched from the top of the slope," she said. "When the smoke got so thick I couldn't see down into the hollow any longer, I left and came back here. I saw them close behind you and then I heard their screams as they tried to fight their way out, only there was no way. The fire was everywhere, ringing everything. Those who weren't burned to death were suffocated by the smoke. It was terrible."

"Didn't expect it would be any other way," Fargo said.

"But you managed to stay alive. You came through it," Emily said. "You put yourself into certain death for me and came out of it. You're something wonderful." He smiled with just the right amount of modesty and Emily ran her hands across his shoulders and chest and hugged him to her again. Suddenly she pulled back and he saw the tiny frown on her brow as her eyes moved across him again. "You don't even smell of smoke," she said. "There's not a smudge of smoke on you, not a charred ash."

He shrugged and tossed her another modest smile. "Lucky, I guess."

The furrow on her brow became a frown. "No, that can't be. You couldn't have fought your way through the flames without even a smudge on you," she said, and her eyes narrowed as she stepped back. "You didn't do that," she said. "You had another way out all along. You never went down there to sacrifice yourself for me. You had an escape hatch ready all along."

"I'm not big on sacrifices," he said.

"Dammit, Fargo, you let me believe you were being a selfless hero," she said. "You let me cry my eyes out, thinking you were burned up with the others."

"A good cry helps the soul," he told her, and caught her wrist as she swung at him.

"Damn you," she hissed. "And you were going to go on letting me think you'd somehow managed to escape."

He let go of her wrist. "You were happy with that. I couldn't take that away from you," he said.

"Damn you."

"It wasn't a cakewalk. Enough happened that I didn't expect," he said. "I damn near didn't get back."

The frown wiped itself from Emily's brow and concern flooded her face. "Sibyl?" she asked.

"Blood is thick. Roots are deep," he said.

She came to him again, her kiss long and tender. "I'm sorry," she said. "You're not completely forgiven, but you're here and that's all that really matters."

"What happens to Emily Holden now?" he asked.

"There's a hospital in Salt Lake. They've wanted me to work for them for a long time," she said. "What will happen to Parasol?"

"The miners and trappers will take over. It won't be

nearly so proper and respectable," Fargo said, "but it'll be a lot more honest."

"I'm tired of respectability and properness. Ride to Salt Lake with me, Fargo," Emily said. "We'll spend every night being very improper but very honest."

"I'd like that," he said, and cupped a hand around her modest breasts.

Salt Lake was far enough away to make for a deliciously improper trip. Everything had its rewards. He smiled in anticipation as Emily gathered her things. The dusk held the promise of the night. The night held the promise of tomorrow. The world went on. Good things waited ahead, and for now, they were all called Emily.

LOOKING FORWARD!
The following is the opening
section from the next novel in the exciting
Trailsman series from Signet:

**THE TRAILSMAN #104
COMANCHE CROSSING**

*Texas, 1860, on the lower Rio Grande,
where bad habits came from Mexico
and left a swath of death and destruction
north to Comanche country . . .*

The big man astride the magnificent black-and-white
pinto stallion rode easy in the saddle under a warm
noonday sun. Not one cloud spoiled the soft blue sky.
The deer path he followed wandered near the north
bank of the lower Rio Grande. He could smell the
lazy-flowing river, although he couldn't see it. Between him and the river shone a blaze of light green
foliage in the sunlight—the springtime colors of mesquite that grew abundantly here and over most of the
state—a plague to ranchers. The low-growing trees
prevented the growth of grass so vital for cattle. In the

sparse open areas among the mesquite were patches of equally prolific prickly-pear, hungry for all the sunlight they could get.

As far as he could see on his right, the flat terrain was a solid dark green with weeds knee high or taller.

After delivering a prize bull to a south Texas rancher, Skye Fargo had headed north. The two-hundred-dollar fee he had received put a small bulge in his left hip pocket. A dull ache in his shoulders was a sore remembrance of the cantankerous bull. The brute had torn down the fence on which Fargo and the rancher had sat to admire the huge animal. Fargo was sent sky-high and landed on his shoulders. But the bull problem was behind him now.

His thoughts centered on his immediate destination, Cougar Canyon, where he could enjoy an interlude on the long journey to the Wyoming Territory. He was due at Fort Laramie the first week of June. Gloria O'Malley, the buxom madam of Rhapsody House in Cougar Canyon, had the absolute biggest copper bathtub west of the Mississippi. Hers was the only tub he'd found that could accommodate his full length.

Well, so could Gloria, but with much grunting and screaming. O'Malley was quick to favor him with her bourbon, her copper tub, and her fleshy body. The mere thought of the curly-haired, redheaded woman brought a grin to his chiseled face, put a twinkle in his lake-blue eyes.

A buzzing hum broke his reverie. The trail meandered through an acre or more of Indian blankets. Legions of bees worked busily among the colorful red, yellow, and brown petals of the pretty wildflowers that resembled blankets made by Indians. The monotonous hum was blissful, almost hypnotic. Fargo couldn't have been more comfortable and at ease if he had ordered it so.

Suddenly the Ovaro raised his head, perked up his ears. Fargo looked up. About a mile away several hillocks interrupted the otherwise level landscape. He reined in to silence the soft sounds of the saddle so his wild-creature hearing could listen through the hum while he studied the hills.

He saw nothing to alert the stallion. Muffled though they were, the dull cracks he heard came from muskets firing up ahead, on the Mexican side of the great river. He spurred the Ovaro to a gallop, left the Indian blankets, and headed for the nearest hill to see what was happening.

Atop the steep rise, he reined to a halt among mesquites. Pulling a limb back to get an unobstructed view, he looked across the river below. Several adobe hovels dotted the barren landscape between the river and the small border town which he recognized as San Miguel, a haven for smugglers and outlaws fleeing Anglo lawmen. The few peons out in the open scampered home. The single dirt street of San Miguel was deserted, standing wide open for easy passage by the four horsemen thundering in from the west.

They rode in a tight diamond formation, pounding hard and fast, heading straight for the river. Less than a hundred yards behind, and closing fast, rode a great force of uniformed *federales* led by an officer on a white horse. The long saber he brandished gleamed in the sunlight, and the soldiers riding in the fore took potshots at the foursome. Fargo presumed they were banditos making for safety in Texas.

As they rode closer, furrows appeared on Fargo's brow, and he raised an eyebrow, for he saw the three in front rode side-saddle. Squinting to bring them into sharper focus, he saw they wore the garb of nuns. A man wearing a brown robe brought up the rear.

Outlaws, smugglers, or no, Fargo didn't cotton to killing women, especially when they were unarmed. He released the branch and withdrew his Sharps from its saddle case. He waited for the soldiers to come within range, then shot the lead musketeer out of the saddle. The fellow fell backward and toppled over the rump of his horse. The pack parted to avoid trampling their comrade tumbling in the swirl of red dust.

As the lead nun's mount plunged into the water at a dead run, Fargo returned the Sharps to its saddle case and started down the mesquite-infested slope. He watched her abandon the saddle most skillfully, but hang onto the saddle horn so the horse could take her across. By the time he reached the base of the hill, dismounted, and got into position to fire from shielding mesquite trees, the other two nuns and the priest were in the river, hanging onto their saddles.

Fargo drew his Colt as the *federales* arrived on the far bank. Now that the clergy had made it into the river—a no man's land, and as such, ostensibly a safe sanctuary—he wouldn't shoot unless the soldiers fired.

He watched the lanky officer to read the man's intentions. The fellow seemed confused as he pranced his horse back and forth along the bank. It was as though he felt unsure what to do next: go after them, let them go free, or have his men shoot them in the water.

Four horsemen, all dressed in white and wearing

white headdresses the likes of which he'd never seen—the head coverings flowed much like bandages unraveling —emerged from behind the troops and rode to the officer. After considerable arm waving, one shouted in bad Spanish to the officer, who nodded.

A decision had been made. On the officer's command, his troops dismounted and formed in two ranks at the river's edge. The front rank knelt and aimed their long-barreled muskets at the foursome in the water. Intentionally bypassing the saber-wielding officer for a more threatening target, Fargo raised the Colt and took aim on a front-line soldier's chest.

The officer shouted, "Fire!"

Ten flintlock hammers fell, igniting powder. Wisps of smoke puffed from the powder holes. A half blink later the muskets roared, belched gunsmoke several feet, and the water around the nuns fairly churned with tiny geysers. Fargo left two of the musketeers sprawling on the bank. As the second rank stepped forward, the front rank stood back to reload. Fargo emptied the cylinder at the replacements, then started reloading.

Infuriated by his men's poor marksmanship and clearly baffled that unarmed swimmers could shoot back, the officer commanded the front rank of soldiers to take good aim and make the river run red with blood. "Fire!" he bellowed.

Again ten muskets belched and missed. Fargo moved his sights from left to right. A bandoleered chest appeared in his sights. He squeezed the trigger and thumbed back the hammer as he crossed to the next target. More bodies littered the bank before the nervous officer spotted Fargo partly hidden by the mesquite.

The swimmers had passed the middle of the stream when the officer pointed his saber at the mesquites and ordered his remaining men to shoot into them. Fargo was finishing reloading as the fusillade of musket balls stripped leaves from branches near him and tore into the hillside. He fired and dropped two musketeers as the lead nun's horse dragged her onto the bank. He shouted to her, "Run to your left! Go behind the hill!"

Ice-blue eyes glanced at him, and she nodded.

He stepped from the veiling mesquite and yelled to the other three, "Hurry! Follow her! *Andale!*"

Fargo shot again as the other two women clambered ashore. They looked at him as they ran alongside their mounts, which he recognized as being Arabians. The priest—who looked as though he might be thirty years old—paused to smile at Fargo and say, "Thank you, *monsieur.*" His voice carried a heavy French accent.

In that instant Fargo heard a ball thud into the man's back and saw him flinch. Fargo dashed to catch him so he wouldn't fall back into the water. Before he got to him, two more balls slammed into the priest's back and knocked him into Fargo's arms. Fargo holstered his Colt, picked up the bleeding man, and ran for safety.

The females were mounted, ready to ride, but dismounted quickly when Fargo rushed up and laid the priest facedown on the ground. To Fargo's surprise the fellow was conscious and alert. The nun with ice-blue eyes pulled the priest's collar open and drew his robe down to expose the wounds. At first sight of the ugly holes, Fargo knew the man had little time left.

In a clear, strong voice, the priest said, *"Monsieur,*

put me on my horse. We must get away from them."
Then he spoke in French to the nun, who Fargo saw
was three, maybe four months pregnant.

She snapped her fingers once. One of the women
instantly took off running back toward the river. Seconds later she returned with the priest's horse. With
the bossy nun's help, Fargo got the priest in his saddle. The man leaned forward, winked at Fargo, then
spurred the Arabian to a gallop. The nuns mounted up
quickly and followed him out of the hills.

Their fast departure left Fargo blinking. Scratching
his head, he whistled for the Ovaro. Ears at attention,
the powerful black-and-white trotted around the hill-
ock to him.

Mounting, he listened to the Mexican officer scream
orders one after another, berating his musketeers for
letting the four escape. Fargo rode just far enough
around the hill to see what the *federales* were up to.
As he watched, the officer led his men down into the
river. Fargo wheeled the stallion, hurried to catch up
with the foursome.

They were threading their way through the mesquite, the Arabians' long tails raised high and whip-
ping. The nuns were damn good riders, maintaining
perfect balance in the side-saddles. The priest was
ahead of them by two lengths.

After breaking out of the trees Fargo caught up with
them. Riding alongside the nuns, he shouted, "Faster,
ladies! The *federales* are coming!"

Nobody so much as glanced his way, but they had
heard his warning. As a unit, the Arabians shot forward. He knew the Ovaro could outrun them on the
short haul, but couldn't stay with them over a long

distance. Arabians were structured for endurance; they could do it all. After running hard for about a half mile, the Arabians pulled away from the tiring pinto. Fargo watched their rumps outdistance him rapidly. He eased back on the pinto's pace and watched the four continue on effortlessly. In less than five minutes they were mere specks, disappearing fast.

Fargo looked behind him to check on the *federales*. They were still picking their way through the thick mesquites, but coming his way. He put the stallion into a canter to cool it down.

An hour passed before Fargo caught sight of the Arabians. They were grazing near a large oak tree. The nuns knelt in the tree's shade. He trotted the Ovaro the rest of the way and reined to a halt near the women. The priest lay facedown on a patch of grass. Fargo eased from the saddle and went to the wounded man.

"*Padre*, I don't know what's keeping you alive," he said. "I will say one thing for you, though. You're a damn tough man."

Fargo looked at the nuns. Were it not for their faces framed by their white wimples, he doubted if he could tell them apart. He decided none of them could be over twenty five. Not a wrinkle showed on any of them, not even a hint of crow's feet. Although they were on their knees, all appeared they would be about the same height—five feet, eight inches—and carried identical weight, no more than a hundred and twenty-five pounds. If the smooth condition of their faces and hands were any indication, the parts he couldn't see under their long habits would prove equally as gorgeous. One had a tiny black mole a half inch from the right corner of her full lips. The nun next to her had dark brown eyes, and bossy, the ice-blue.

Fargo singled out Ice-Blue and said, "There's a canteen hanging on my saddle horn. Would you bring it to me?"

Her fingers snapped twice. Brown Eyes went and fetched the canteen. He remembered the earlier snap had triggered Tiny Mole to fetch the priest's horse. Ice-Blue had them trained to move on finger snaps; one and two obviously meant "fetch." He wondered what three snaps meant.

Fargo turned the priest's head to one side and put the rim of the canteen to his mouth, but the priest refused to drink. He cut his eyes to Fargo's, both urgency and pleading in them. The man was dying and trying to tell him something with his eyes before death came.

Fargo realized he wanted to speak, but didn't have the strength left to get the words out. He removed his hat and bent his left ear close to the priest's mouth. The words came haltingly, barely discernible in the man's waning breaths. "*Monsieur* . . . I beg you . . . take them . . . a place . . ." The priest gasped as his eyes closed.

Fargo reckoned the man had taken his final breath, but the priest wasn't dead yet, only catching his wind. His eyes fluttered open, and this time Fargo strained to hear the words carried in the soft breathing. "Promise me you will protect them . . . take them . . . Cowtown."

"I know the place. I promise I will," Fargo whispered.

The dying man half smiled, then continued. "They hold a secret, *monsieur* . . . must protect. Beware Achmid, *monsieur* . . . al . . . cazara . . ."

"Al what?" Fargo whispered.

But the priest's ears could no longer hear. Neither did his dark eyes have vision. Fargo dragged two fingers down over the eyelids to close them, then rocked back on his haunches and looked south. The *federales* were a mile or more away, riding as doggedly as before. He shifted his gaze to the three immobile faces. "We must leave," he began. "There isn't enough time to bury him here. Do we take the body and have it slow us down, or do we leave him here in the shade for the *federales* to find?"

There was no consultation among the nuns, not even an exchange of glances. Neither did any of them so much as cut her eyes at the dead priest. Ice-Blue replied in a husky, authoritative voice, "We leave Father Jeansonne." Without any snapping of her fingers the trio rose, went to their horses, and mounted up.

Fargo silently agreed with her wisdom. At the same time he felt a mild shudder ripple through his body, for his sixth sense warned him these women were cold-blooded, especially Ice-Blue in whose veins ice water surely flowed.

Without looking back at the priest, Fargo got in his saddle and headed the Ovaro northeast at a gallop. The nuns rode in a line abreast of him.

Shortly before sundown, they left the flatness of the lower Rio Grande valley and entered rolling hill country. Within half an hour, Fargo found a spring-fed pond among large rocks. He reined to a halt beside a large boulder and told them, "We camp here for the night. No fire, though. Find a place to spread your bedrolls. I'll stand guard till midnight, then one of you can spell me. Who do I awaken?"

In an accent that matched the dead French priest's, Ice-Blue answered immediately, "Awaken me, *monsieur*."

"Er, uh, how will I know which is you?" he stammered.

She looked at a tight space between two rocks. "There. I sleep light. I will hear you coming."

He nodded and said, "My name's Skye Fargo. What do I call each of you?"

Ice-Blue glanced at Tiny Mole. "Sister Monique." Looking at Brown Eyes, she said, "Sister Camille. I am Sister Andrea. *Monsieur*, is it safe for us to bathe?"

He looked at her and checked a frown trying to form. They were cold-blooded, all right, he thought. Their priest lies dead under the oak, *federales* bent on murdering them are breathing down their necks, and they want to take a bath. "Of course you're safe," he answered dryly. He wondered if he were safe. Sisters Camille and Monique were eyeing him the way a fox eyes hens trapped in a henhouse. Nuns weren't supposed to do that. He got his Sharps and scaled the tallest boulder to sit and keep guard.

Fargo watched the trio spread their bedrolls, then inspect their horses' hooves. He thought Sister Monique had the best-looking Arabian. The gelding, a bay, had a black mane and tail, and a beautifully arched, long, fine neck. Sister Camille's mount, also a gelding, was jet-black. Sister Andrea rode a chestnut mare. All appeared to stand about fourteen and a tad hands tall. Satisfied with the condition of the hooves, they walked to the pond.

While they were in dark shadows, he could still see them only vaguely, not clearly enough to discern Sister

Andrea's belly. They didn't seem concerned that he sat in clear sight of them. Their uncaring made him a mite uncomfortable. Fargo wondered what all went on inside those back rooms of missions late at night. He turned so he wasn't facing them directly. Nonetheless, he caught himself watching them out the corners of his eyes several times while they undressed and entered the water. He knew the spring-fed pond was ice-cold, but not one of them so much as uttered a low whimper, or gasped, or gave any indication she felt it.

"I was right," he muttered to himself, "all three are cold-blooded."

Fargo shifted his gaze to the majestic red disk of the setting sun and frowned. Framed by the fiery curvature was the silhouette of a hill. On top of the hill stood six mounted riders, none of whom wore the tall, easy-to-recognize hats he'd seen on the *federales*.

Beyond and left of the hill licked the first flames of a campfire. He watched it for a moment and mused aloud, "The *federales* are cooking supper."

As the red rim vanished, he looked toward the hilltop again. The horsemen had also disappeared. He wondered if they had spotted him.

Fargo looked down on the pond, now obscured by darkness, thankful for the nuns' discipline at maintaining silence.

A coyote howled.

Through the mournful cry he heard a hammer fall behind him.